MORE THAN A FLING

BOOK THREE OF THE HEARTLAND SERIES

JILL DOWNEY

More Than A Fling

The Heartland Series
Book 3

by
Jill Downey

DEDICATION

In gratitude I dedicate this third novel to my first
teachers... my family... four legged and two...

Who taught me about acceptance, intimacy, inclusion...

And most importantly about love.

CHAPTER 1

*A*nnie Morgan loved springtime and the change of seasons that living in the heartland of Michigan provided. The weather was certainly rolling out the red carpet for her sister Darcy's flight today. It was a pristine day with temperatures hovering around seventy degrees, sunny skies, and billowing white clouds floating above. The scenic drive displayed the best of Michigan's spring spectacle, teasing their senses with breathtaking beauty. The flowering magnolias and forsythias along with the apricot trees all united to be some of the first to exhibit their colorful blooms and delightful fragrances.

"You've got your passport?" Annie asked.

"Yep. By the way, I signed up for an international plan for my cell, which wasn't that expensive, so I'll have use of my phone while I'm there," Darcy said.

"Cool. Now I'll have to remember the six-hour time difference. You'll be ahead right?"

"Yep."

"Promise you'll take a gazillion pictures."

"Promise."

"Swear to me that you'll throw a coin in the Trevi Fountain. Remember, keep your back to the fountain, coin in right hand, toss over your left shoulder." Annie said as she turned into the long lane leading back to the farm owned by Sam Parker, Darcy's fiancée and fellow traveler.

"You crack me up. Superstitious much?"

"I mean it."

"Okay, yes, I swear. Geesh," Darcy said.

"Legend has it, if you throw three coins in the fountain, you'll be guaranteed a return trip to Rome, a love affair, and the third coin brings marriage."

"Now it's three coins? Since they are your coins I'll be throwing, will it be your luck or mine?" Darcy asked.

"Doesn't seem like too much effort to go through for that big a payoff. If I were you, I'd throw three in for yourself, after you toss mine in." Annie grinned at her older sister knowing that she was skeptical of the unprovable, but she also knew Darcy would follow through just in case.

"I can't believe it's finally happening; when Sam and I first started planning for this vacation, we thought this day would never get here," Darcy said.

"I know. You so deserve this time off. Sam too. After everything you both went through last year, a month is probably not long enough," Annie said.

"I've never had a month off in my entire adult life," Darcy said.

"And to spend it in Italy, *Bellissima*. Totally on my list of top ten places to visit before I die," Annie said. "Did you pack your journal?"

"I brought a small notebook, and I'm going to write something every single day, even if it's only a sentence or two."

"Good."

As they pulled up, Sam came bounding down the stairs, his face lit with excitement.

"Where the hell have you been?" Sam said.

Glancing at her wristwatch Annie said, "What do you mean? We're early."

"I've been packed and ready for two hours."

"Your problem, not ours." Annie loved Sam. He was like the big brother she never had.

They all turned when they heard a male voice say, "Hey, you weren't going to leave without saying goodbye were ya?"

Annie knew exactly who that sexy voice belonged to: Gabe Hunter. She blushed slightly at the sight of him, her senses suddenly on high alert. He was even more gorgeous than she had remembered. "Hi Gabe."

"Damn, if it isn't Annie Morgan. My God! Where the hell have you been all my life?"

"Right under your nose." She smiled green eyes sparkling. "You are looking mighty fine there, cowboy."

Gabe clutched at his heart and reeled comically as if he'd been struck.

"Quit flirting and grab one of my bags," Sam said.

"Aye-aye boss."

What a body! Annie watched as he took the steps two at a time and returned a moment later with a duffle bag and a small carry-on. He stowed it in the hatch of the VW.

"Gabe, I gave you Darcy's number, if you need me don't hesitate to call," Sam said.

"Go. Forget about everything here. That's why you pay me the big bucks. Everything will be fine, so quit worrying."

"I have total faith in you, or I wouldn't consider being gone for a week let alone a month." Most of Sam's energy was directed toward his veterinarian practice; as farm manager, Gabe kept things running smoothly.

"It's going to be quiet around here without you," Gabe said.

"You will be too busy to miss anyone," Sam said, laughing as he got into the back seat of the car.

Gabe walked over to Annie's car window and leaned down to her level, "Hey, it's really great to see you again."

"Yeah for me too. Maybe I'll see you around, cowboy."

"I hope so."

"Have fun guys, and Sam don't forget the Trevi fountain," Gabe called as Annie pulled away.

Annie caught her sister's eye, grinning from ear to ear, "See, it's not just me, everyone knows about wishing wells and destiny."

*S*he pulled off the four-lane highway following the signs, leaving the countryside behind as they arrived at the airport terminal with plenty of time to spare. She carefully merged with the congested traffic of fellow travelers who were trying to catch flights or arriving to pick up loved ones. Annie honked her horn as a Hummer narrowly missed her front bumper while cutting in front of them.

"Damn, that was close," Darcy said. "Pull in

anywhere you can find a spot, we can take it from there."

"You guys are going to have so much fun. This is the trip of a lifetime. The only downside is that you will be missing out on our most beautiful time of the year here," Annie said.

"I think I can handle that," Darcy replied.

"Me too," Sam said

"Yeah, I won't waste my pity on either of you," Annie said.

She managed to squeeze into a spot by the curb and put on her flashers. Jumping out for last minute hugs, and to unload their bags from the hatch, she suddenly wished it was her leaving instead of them. It was so hard to be the one left behind. "Make sure you call me after you land," Annie said.

"I will. Take good care of my babies," Darcy said, tearing up a little at the thought of leaving her three pit bull companions. They loved their Aunt Annie, but they would miss her while she was away.

"Don't worry about a thing sis," Annie said reassuringly, "They could be like most of the canines in similar circumstances, sitting in a kennel wondering what the hell happened—instead they get me as a roommate for a month."

"I know you'll spoil them rotten," Darcy said.

"As if..." she said referring to their already spoiled existence.

"Okay then, you be good. Please be careful and alert. I'm not convinced that Bradley has given up on a reconciliation." Grabbing the handle of her luggage, she pulled Annie in for one last hug.

"Will you quit worrying? Go and have the time of

your life. You deserve this more than anybody, I mean it." Annie said. She used her sleeve to wipe the welling tears away. "I'm going to miss you guys."

"The time will fly, and before you know it, I'll be back home bossing you around like always." Darcy's eyes were suspiciously bright, mirroring her sister's.

"Come on babe, we've got to go," Sam urged.

"Bye!"

"See you in a month."

"Have fun."

Annie watched them until they disappeared through the airport entrance. An overwhelming loneliness descended upon her for a moment until she willfully shook it off. Pulling back into the fray of vehicles, she headed to her salon for a full day of back-to-back hair appointments.

CHAPTER 2

*A*nnie sighed as she hung up the phone after managing to squeeze a cut and color into her overbooked schedule. You would have thought they were trying to set up a meeting between royalty, everyone's lives were so busy these days.

Her hair salon, The Diamond, was in its fourth year of operation and thriving. She had recently added a fourth stylist and was currently paying for the training of her second nail tech, Rachel. She also had a licensed massage therapist who worked by appointment and an esthetician who was in high demand.

Success had a price though, and lately Annie felt like her life was out of balance...all work and no play. Fortunately, it was Wednesday, and she only had two more days to wait until she would be taking off for a whole weekend of fun at the lake with friends. It was sure to be a wild weekend celebrating her friend's upcoming wedding.

Gabe Hunter. Damn. She couldn't believe she had

run into him today. He was too sexy for his own good and for hers as well. The attraction she had felt for him last year, rather than diminishing, had dialed up a decimal or two. She was pretty sure he had felt the heat as well.

That day they had spent together last fall had been magical. Horses, a great guy, beautiful weather...there had been an immediate attraction between them. Unfortunately, the timing had been all wrong—she in the process of disentangling from Bradley, and he already in a relationship.

Gabe's movie-star good looks and easy-going style might be a bit much to handle. She was certain that women gravitated toward him like bears to honey. Charming and funny, he had been just what the doctor ordered that day, but it would be a challenge to feel secure in a relationship with him when he was so damn compelling. Anyway, it was of no concern to her. She had sworn off men after ending a disastrous relationship with her cop-boyfriend Bradley.

Currently Annie was focused on her career, friends, and family, and hoped to fit in a few of her old pastimes, like horseback riding and hiking. Those days of freedom, when she could take to the woods by horseback or on foot almost daily, seemed so far away. Now she was lucky if she could squeeze in a hike two days a week.

Annie looked around with a feeling of contentment and pleasure for her accomplishments and success with the salon, but her greatest satisfaction came from the sense of family and comradery they all shared. She loved the hubbub and chatter, the laughter and tears, the sense of community; they truly had one another's backs, and that was priceless as far as Annie was concerned. Annie was completely unaware of how well she wore her contentment. The tense and tight expression she had worn for so long while dating Bradley was now replaced with a soft and relaxed countenance. Her whole body exuded ease and happiness, which only enhanced her stunning beauty.

The door jingled and Annie looked up to see Rachel, her nail tech-in-training, enter the salon with two kids in tow, one holding her hand, and the other balanced on her hip.

"Hey Annie, I hope you don't mind, I had to bring the kids with me, but my mom is picking them up here in about fifteen minutes. She was running behind, and I didn't want to be late getting here to cover the phones for you," she said, looking extremely frazzled.

"No problem, my client isn't even here yet," Annie said.

Rachel's little boy was two and a half, and her baby girl almost a year old now. She had her hands full as a single parent and all of them at the salon had adopted the family. Everyone was willing to help to make sure that Rachel's dreams could become a reality.

As part of their arrangement, Rachel worked part-time filling in as a receptionist, greeting customers, taking phone calls and scheduling appointments.

It was a life saver for Annie, and it gave Rachel a little extra money while she learned about the business and completed her certificate in cosmetology.

Annie held out her arms toward Cara and was immediately rewarded with two chubby arms reaching back and a smile that lit up the room.

"Come here you little munchkin," Annie said to the

adorable little girl with blond ringlet curls and a pink bow in her hair. Holding her close she pressed her nose into the child's hair, savoring that baby smell.

She walked over to her styling station to let Cara look at all the tempting wares of the trade, eyes huge round saucers as she opened and closed tight fists, reaching for anything she could get her hands on.

"Are you going to come work for me when you grow up little one?" Annie said. She laughed at the comical expression on Cara's face as she concentrated on Annie's hair. "You are so cute I could eat you up," Annie said.

The other two stylists, who currently had customers in their salon chairs, looked on with amusement.

"When are you going to settle down and have a couple of your own?" June asked Annie as she placed another piece of foil in her client's hair and painted on the color.

"Hey. I've got plenty of time. I still haven't hit the big three-oh yet," she said laughing.

"You will this year though… goodbye twenties," June said.

"Look who is talking, didn't you step over to the other side last month? I don't see any gaggle of kid's hanging on to your coattails yet."

"Who has the time? I'm having way too much fun. Kids would definitely cramp my style."

"That's what I'm saying." Zoey the other stylist chimed in as she guided her client to the rinsing bowl.

The door jingled again and this time it was James, their only male stylist, arms loaded down with packages.

"Please tell me that you didn't empty the store

again," Annie said. It was a joke amongst the salon employees that James was obsessed with interior design and a compulsive shopper. However, he was damn good at decorating and had a naturally artistic eye.

"It was bargain city... I mean who could resist. The sale was fabulous, darling

"Let's see what you bought," Zoey said. Now everyone's interest was piqued including the clients' as he began to unpack his latest acquisitions.

"This is divine." he said pulling out a diamond mirror ball lamp, attached to a silver chain. Everyone agreed and made noises of appreciation for his choice.

"Wait until you see this lit up. I'm going to have William hang it up over my station this weekend," he said referring to his partner of fifteen years.

"Hey, if he's going to be here anyway do you think he could fix my shelf? It's becoming a liability," Zoey said.

"I'm sure he would be happy to," James said.

There was a flurry of activity as Rachel's mom arrived to retrieve the kids and Annie's client showed up all at the same time. The children squawked at having to leave such an exciting environment, but grandma had been prepared, and her bribe of ice cream cones had done the trick as they quickly abandoned their protest and happily exited... on to their next adventure.

Annie's client consulted with her about different haircuts and styles. After some discussion on what cut would best suit her features, Annie wielded the scissors with confidence and began to clip away.

"You know I've been thinking about chopping my

own hair off," Annie shared, only to be met by a cacophony of protests from everyone in the salon.

"Nooooo! You have the most gorgeous hair of anyone I have ever met," Zoey said, truly aghast at the suggestion.

"I won't let you," June said.

"Why would you tamper with perfection?" James said.

"I guess I'll have to go elsewhere or do it myself when the time comes, since I obviously have no support from any of you."

"You got that right." Zoey said.

"It all depends...you would have to convince me and find the perfect cut. Of course, you would be gorgeous even if we shaved your entire head," James said.

"There is hope then. I knew I could count on you J.J.," she said using the endearment.

"Oh, she pulled the J.J. card out. I guess we know who is sucking up to the boss and it appears to be working," Zoey said.

Annie smiled and winked at her customer, who enjoyed the easy banter amongst friends. It was a good day.

"Why don't you let me shape and tint your brows today," Annie suggested.

"Sure," her client agreed.

"I also think we should go a little blonder with your hair this time since it's almost summer," Annie recommended. She stepped back to get a different perspective of her handiwork with the scissors, concentrating intently on her subject.

"I was thinking the same thing," she said.

James walked over to the two of them, studied

Annie's client and offered his opinion, "If it were me darling, I would go short, as in pixie. With your beautiful heart-shaped face and huge eyes, it will frame your face beautifully."

"Oh my God. That thought is terrifying," her client said.

"You know I think he is right…it would look great on you," Annie said encouragingly.

Zoey and June both chimed in their agreement.

"So, we now have a consensus… that is, if you are on board," Annie said. "Super short with bangs, razor cut edges, platinum blond, dark brows, what do you think?" she said now excited at the prospect of creating a whole new look for her client.

"Why not live dangerously," she said bravely.

"Yay. I think you will love it," Annie said.

"It will be absolutely divine darling," James concurred.

"Let's do it."

Two hours later her client walked out of the salon completely transformed. She would be another walking advertisement for The Diamond.

"Thanks, ya'll. That was what you would call a team effort," Annie said cheerfully. "She loved it, good call J.J. she complimented her fellow stylist.

"Don't mention it," he waved his hand at her. "She is a knockout, and now she looks as if she stepped out of Vogue Magazine."

"That was so much fun. Reminds me of why I got into this business," Annie said.

"Folks, I'm officially done for the day," Zoey said, as she finished organizing her station.

"I think we're all heading out," James replied.

"See you tomorrow, I won't be in until eleven, then I work straight through until eight o'clock," Zoey shared.

"I'm pulling a ten-hour shift tomorrow starting at nine, with a long break to take care of my sister's fur babies," Annie said.

"I can come in and work the front desk for a couple of hours tomorrow if you need me to," Rachel said.

"Yes!" they all chorused at the same time.

Laughing Rachel said shyly, "It feels good to be so popular."

"Are you kidding me? I am not sure how we even functioned before you came along," Annie said giving her a big hug. "I'll lock up, I've got a couple more things to do before I head out," she said. "Rachel, I'll leave the keys to Darcy's house and the alarm combination in the petty cash drawer when I leave the salon on Friday. Thanks so much for house-sitting for me this weekend. It saved my butt," she said rolling her eyes

"Are you sure you don't want me to wait for you Annie?" J.J. said, protective of her after her troubles with the ex.

"Nope I'll be fine you worrywart, I haven't seen or heard a peep from Bradley for over a month," she said reassuringly.

"If you're sure darlin'...I guess I'll go, love you," he said.

"I love you too J.J., see you tomorrow."

After finishing up with a few last-minute details she gathered up her things, turning out the lights she locked the door behind her. She was struggling with the lock in the fading light when a male voice startled her, and she shrieked as she dropped her keys.

"Bradley, you scared me to death! What in the world are you doing here?"

"I was on my way home, just got off duty...I miss you Annie. I was hoping we could talk," he said. He was still in his police uniform.

"We have already been over this, the answer is still the same, N-O," she spelled out. "Our agreement was that you stay away from me," she reminded him.

Seeing Bradley again was beyond difficult. He was as sexy as ever with his dark almost-black eyes and black hair, not to mention his killer body, but she knew she couldn't go down that path again. It made her sad.

It had been good in the beginning, and she had lived on those crumbs for many months, before finally admitting that his dark passenger was really the one in charge. She had given him more chances than he deserved, and his behavior had escalated the previous fall from slightly erratic to completely unpredictable. She was pleased to note that she really had moved on; she could tell because she wasn't even slightly tempted to engage with him.

"Annie can you honestly say that you don't miss me too?" He reached as if to touch her face then let his hand drop. "I love you Annie," he said again.

"I can't say that I don't think of the good times, however it doesn't change anything," she said firmly. "We're bad for each other and I can't trust you."

"Baby, I've changed...I'll do anything, I mean that— therapy, give up drinking," voice breaking, "I can't go on without you, my life isn't worth a shit without you in it, please give me another chance," he pleaded.

"Bradley you have to move on, and so do I. It's over,"

she said. She fought her impulse to comfort him in his obvious emotional anguish.

Sensing her weakness, he pushed again, "Annie, remember how it used to be with us? How can you let that all go? We were so good together, Baby, let me make it up to you. I promise, no more anger, no more fighting, just us making love, having fun like we used to, will you at least think about it?"

"I have thought about it, and that is why we're not together. It wasn't like I didn't care about you, leaving you was the hardest thing I've ever had to do, but you know as well as I do that it wasn't only the 'fighting.'"

"I know I was a jerk and I hate that I took you for granted."

"Bradley, that was the least of it. I can handle conflict and even a good fight now and then, but with you it was constant criticism, the unpredictability of your emotions, your flying into rages for no apparent reason. I can't trust that the minute you had me back you won't return to your old ways. I've been slowly putting my life back together, I'm sorry," she said gently.

A car came screeching to a halt a few feet away from where they stood, "What the hell are you doing here?" J.J. said shouting from inside of his car. He had decided to drive back around to check on Annie. Seeing Bradley there, he was glad that he had.

"It's all right J.J., Bradley was just leaving. Weren't you Bradley?" Annie said." J.J. got out of the car and stood between Annie and Bradley arms crossed, eyes blazing mad.

"You heard her, she said she's fine," Bradley said arrogantly. "You can get back in your car and drive off to your Partner," he said condescendingly using his fingers as quotation marks.

"Fuck you Brad, get out of here or I'll call one of your buddies to come and get you," James replied.

"Go Bradley, this conversation is over," Annie said.

"I'm going, but please, think about what I said." He shot a quick glare at James which immediately morphed into a long-suffering look towards Annie as he departed.

"You need to file a restraining order Annie," James said.

"Why, so he can lose his job and become more desperate?"

"That's on him not you," he said.

"I can't do that. He would lose everything, and honestly it would probably make things even worse for me."

"That guy is a nut job, and I'm afraid of what he's capable of," he said.

"I'm tired, I want to go home," Annie said. "He won't bother me any more tonight, and as an added bonus, he doesn't know I'm staying at my sister's. Plus, he's trying to prove that he is a changed man, I'll be fine," Annie said firmly. "Go home to William, please, I'm not scared, a little rattled is all."

"I can come over for a little while," James said.

"No, I promise, I'm good, thanks anyway."

"Are you sure"

"Yes, I'm sure."

"I am going to follow you home, I'll call William and tell him I'll be a couple of minutes late, no arguments from you," he said.

"That is an offer I'll gladly accept."

CHAPTER 3

Friday finally arrived, and the excitement ran high as everyone piled out of the rental van to gape at the beautiful view of the lake. The six women had brought enough luggage for their two-night stay to clothe an army. They had stopped at the local grocery store and loaded up on food and beverages.

"Oh my God. This view is incredible. You did good Annie," Abigail said.

"Wait until you see the inside, it's spectacular," Annie replied.

They all grabbed grocery bags and the ice they had purchased and began unloading the van.

"It's got four bedrooms so a couple of us will have to share," Annie said. "Since Abbey is the bride, she gets the master suite. I'm happy to share a room with someone," Annie volunteered.

"I'll be your roomy, if you aren't already sick of me," Zoey said.

"I was thinking the same thing," Annie said giving her a quick reassuring hug. "I could never get sick of you. That's settled then."

They all explored the lake house, then unloaded the luggage into their respective bedrooms. When Annie returned to the main living area, she opened the sliding glass doors that extended over the entire wall and showcased the spectacular lake view. Water as far as the eye could see. They had a deck, complete with a hot-tub, lounge chairs, and a dining table with a bright orange umbrella. Linda and Ava had returned to the kitchen and began putting groceries away while Evelyn opened a bottle of wine.

"This is truly heaven on earth," Linda said appreciatively. "I could park my ass right here and never leave for the entire weekend," she claimed.

"Too bad, you are going to go out partying with us whether you want to or not," Ava threatened.

"Spoil sport," she said sticking out her tongue.

"Yes, I have the limo rented and it's picking us up at seven. It's all planned out, attendance is mandatory," Annie said. "I have reservations for dinner, then we'll hit several bars, the last one has live music, a country band, and they are supposed to be really good," Annie shared.

"I can't wait," Madison exclaimed.

They all took their drinks to the deck and scattered around eager and ready to get the party started.

~

*T*he bouncer checked all their IDs before allowing them to enter into the noisy fray with the opening band in full swing. The six women made quite an entrance when they walked into their last stop of the evening, a huge honkytonk bar and music venue. They practically represented the whole color spectrum of hair and skin, from Annie's fair complexion and red mane to Ava's pretty pecan skin tones and dark brunette hair. This, along with their varying heights, Abigail the tallest at 5'9, to Zoey's petite 5'3, caused everyone's heads to turn as they entered.

Annie, already tipsy, pulled Ava along with her onto the dance floor. She immediately began whooping it up to the band's cover of "Boot Scootin' Boogie."

Annie's white sleeveless crop top exposed more than a little of her toned torso, and she had paired it with a mid-thigh black tube skirt which fit her like a glove. Completing the sexy ensemble were her silver-studded black leather cowboy boots. In honor of country music, she had brought along her cowboy hat for fun.

It didn't take long before a couple of men, emboldened by alcohol, decided sidle up as close as they could to Annie and Ava on the dance floor. The women did their best to ignore them and concentrate on each other, but one of the men was particularly persistent which led them to give up on the dancing to find the rest of the girls. They decided to wait until the main act to try again.

"Come on, one shot," Zoey insisted.

"No. You will have to carry me out," Annie protested.

Abbey insisted, "Come on! This is my bachelorette party. How about a shot of peach schnapps?"

Everyone agreed to that and they toasted the bride-to-be before downing the fiery liquid. By this time the main act was taking the stage, so they all decided to claim their spot on the dance floor so as not to get crowded out. The bar was packed, and the crowd was pumped, noisy, and full of life. There was a healthy representation of all ages from twenty-somethings to sixty-somethings.

Laughing together over the noise and chaos, they huddled expectantly as the band took their places on stage and introduced themselves.

"Hey ya'll we want to thank you for coming out to hear us, we call ourselves The Lonesome Cowpokes, and we are excited to play for you tonight," the lead singer said.

Annie's mouth fell open as she suddenly realized that the man behind the microphone was none other than Gabe Hunter. She felt dizzy for a moment and her heart started racing as she gazed at the gorgeous man who had begun to sing the iconic bar-tune favorite, "Friends in Low Places" to rousing cheers from the audience.

"Are you alright Annie?" Abbey said noticing that her friend suddenly looked like she had seen a ghost.

"Yes, I think I am. Remember that guy I told you about last year, the one who was on that trail ride?"

"Yeah, so?"

"That's him...the one singing," she said.

"Whoa mama. You weren't kidding when you said he was gorgeous." she said admiringly. "Let's see, he's a cowboy, handsome, and now we know that he's also a musician...every girl's fantasy."

"Way out of my league," Annie said.

"Are you kidding me? You're out of his league. You are a freak you're so perfect," she said. "If you weren't such a great person, I would hate you," Abbey joked, yelling over the music. By this time the whole crowd was singing along to the fun tune and Annie and Ava joined in, belting it out with the best of them. "Chases my blues away..." they sang.

The band easily segued from the bar favorite into a classic Allman Brothers tune, "Sweet Melissa." Annie closed her eyes to filter out the distraction of Gabe, enabling her to get into the song. Her body swayed sensually to the rhythm, as she let the music carry her away. She loved this song and he displayed incredible vocals and his guitar picking wasn't too shabby either. They were good.

She opened her eyes for a quick peek at the stage and was startled to find Gabe staring at her with a burning intensity. As they locked gazes, he missed a beat, quickly recovering, he smiled at her with a thousand-watt grin and a wink that zapped her like a taser. As she smiled back, she was jostled by the same guy that had been hitting on her before. *Here we go again, and now he appeared to be even more inebriated.*

With slurred speech, he demanded, "Hey beautiful, dance with me." He grabbed at her waist trying to pull her into his arms.

Annie, not too stable herself, lost her balance as she tried to pull away from him. "Um, no, I'm here with my friends, thanks anyway," she said trying to let him down nicely.

"I'm not taking no for an answer," he said. He obviously had a high opinion of himself and his ability to convince her to succumb to his dubious charms.

"Please, I said no," she repeated.

"What, you think you are too good for me?" he snarled as he thrust his pelvis crudely against her.

Suddenly the singing stopped as Gabe jumped off the stage to intervene. Grabbing the guy by his shirt, he pulled him through the crowd and away from Annie saying, "I think the lady was pretty clear that she's not interested in your attention."

"Fuck you, I think it's none of your damn business," he said.

Gabe kept a tight grip on the jerk and on his own temper as he steered him toward the exit. The bouncer, alerted by the musical break, met Gabe and took over from there, kicking the guy out of the club.

Gabe easily jumped back up onto the stage and said, "My apologies for the interruption, now let's get back to the music." Annie stood there slightly dazed, trying to wrap her head around what had happened.

"OMG." Zoey said. "What the hell was that? It was like a romantic scene from a movie," she sighed. "I think our lead singer has the hots for you."

"No, we met before, he's best friends with my sister's fiancée, Sam," she said.

"You could have fooled me...that had nothing to do with your sister or Sam—that was all about you my friend," she said. "He's definitely into you."

"Don't be ridiculous," Annie said, feeling her cheeks get hot.

"You know that you're blushing, don't you?"

"I need another drink. Let's head to the bar," she replied.

In truth, it was probably the last thing she needed, she acknowledged to herself, but…when in Rome.

CHAPTER 4

Several songs later the band took a break and Gabe headed straight toward Annie.

"Annie," he said, devouring her with his smoldering eyes.

"Gabe, I was shocked to see you up on stage!" she said. She felt a tingly warmth in her groin and her immediate and intense reaction to this man was a new experience for Annie.

He really was beautiful. The natural sun-streaks of blond in his brown hair looked like they had been applied by a paint brush dipped in gold, rivaling any salon touch-ups. His light brown eyes had flecks of gold and were surrounded by thick dark lashes and brows. He was ruggedly handsome, in that bad-boy kind of way. Dangerous!

"My God Annie! I couldn't wait for the set to finish. I can't believe you are here, in the flesh and blood instead of floating around in my fantasies," Gabe said. "I've been thinking about you. Our trail ride, and then seeing you the other day, I just…I don't know, maybe it's fate."

"Trevi," she said slurring ever-so- slightly.

"What did you say? Trevi?"

"Never mind, it's nothing," Annie said, then giggled. "You're really good, I mean…um…your singing…" she hiccupped, "You know what I mean, so's your band. You could go pro, I'm sure of it," she said.

"So, what brings you all the way up here?" he asked, since it was about an hour away from their hometown.

"Bridal party, the wedding's next week and I'm the maid of honor, so any excuse…" she smiled flirtatiously, her dimples on full display. She looked up at him through her lashes, finally finding her footing despite being tipsy.

"Annie, I have to get back on stage, but I want to get your number before you leave, that is, if you're interested in getting together sometime. Are you seeing anyone?"

"No, but what about your girlfriend?" she asked.

"We broke up soon after that ride. Wanted different things. I'm single, unattached, available, and hopeful," he said.

"Hopeful?"

"Hopeful that you'll say yes."

"Yes," she hiccupped then giggled, beginning to feel the full effects of all the alcohol she had consumed.

"It's so good to see you, I'm glad you're here," he said.

"Me too. Gabe you're so hot," she said, inhibitions now out the window. She put her hand on his chest to balance herself and he sucked his breath in sharply.

Staring hungrily into her eyes he replied, "You must

be looking through your beer goggles. I'll catch you after the last set." He left and returned to the stage.

Annie and her group all gathered on the dance floor and stayed there enjoying the musical mix of southern rock, along with contemporary and classic country. As the band sang their encore song, Annie's head spun, and she knew she had passed several drinks too many. Signaling to her friends that she was ready to leave, they headed to the door, Gabe caught up with her.

"Hey, I'm devastated that you were going to leave without giving me your number," he said.

"I left it with the bouncer," she said, "but hey, now that you are here, want to walk me to our limo?" She hung on tight to Gabe's arm since her legs felt wobbly.

He glanced back at the band who were tearing down and said, "Sure."

Annie's friends were already piled into the limo when she and Gabe reached the vehicle, so they had a moment to themselves. She put her arms around Gabe's neck. "You're so hot," she said, standing on her tip toes, she kissed him lightly on the lips as her hat toppled off her head onto the ground.

"Oh Annie, you make it so hard to say no" he said, returning the kiss he pressed his lips to hers. The minute their mouths met it was as if someone had put a match to the campfire kindling. She moved her hands to his chest, loving the feel of his hard, muscled body beneath her fingertips. *Hard, lean, strong.*

He pulled away then leaned his forehead against hers whispering in a ragged voice, "Talk about zero to sixty, wow Annie, you could pretty much get me to do about anything your sweet little heart desires right about now. Best you go easy on me. I'm too young to die of a broken heart," his husky voice conveying his arousal. "I'd better get back in there, or my band will begin to wonder what happened to me."

He brushed her hair back from her brow and kissed her forehead. His wandering lips found the curve between her neck and shoulder and he nipped lightly, her floral scented skin arousing him even further.

"I'll call you," he said, reluctantly releasing her.

"Promise?" she asked her eyes glazed with passion.

"Promise." After brushing his nose lightly across hers, he picked up her hat from the ground and put it back on her head. He opened the limo door and she climbed in with her friends for their ride home.

"Lord have mercy, that man is fine," Ava said, as they pulled away.

"I am officially jealous," Evelyn said.

"I'm officially depressed," Linda said.

"You guys, what am I going to do? I just got my life back together, the last thing I need is to complicate it with a man," Annie moaned.

Madison said, "I'll take him."

"What about Craig?" Annie said.

"Craig who?" she responded, and they all laughed.

"Quit fretting, you haven't even gone out with the guy yet," Abigail said.

"It feels different, I don't know how to explain it, but I've never felt quite like this with any other guy before," she admitted reluctantly.

"Remember, there was alcohol involved so don't sweat it yet," Zoey said offering an explanation.

"Good point," Annie said relieved that she had an

excuse for her overwhelming reaction to seeing Gabe again.

"I'm going straight to bed when we get home," Annie said.

"I'm going to read all day and hopefully finish my book," Linda said.

"I'm up for kayaking if anyone wants to join me," Zoey said.

"Me," Abbey said.

"Me too," echoed Madison.

"Me three," Ava added. "Evelyn what about you?"

"R & R one hundred percent," she said adamantly. "I volunteer to fix our dinner, those of us staying behind can work on that while you're on the water."

"Perfect," Zoey said, "I hate cooking."

The rest of the ride was silent as they all dozed off lulled by the quiet and smooth ride of the limo.

~

Gabe and his band mates sat down at the bar for a cold beer after loading up their equipment.

"Hey dude, didn't know you were a descendant of Sir Lancelot," Jake ribbed his friend.

"Yeah, what was that all about?" Derek asked.

"That was about one beautiful woman," Nate said interjected.

"Hey, that guy was getting way too aggressive and I couldn't let it go by without stepping in before it went too far," Gabe said. "By the way, her name is Annie, we met last year at the farm. I was still with Sydney at the time," he shared, and they all collectively groaned at the mention of his ex-girlfriend.

"Man, she is bee-you-tee-ful," Derek said admiringly.

"That she is, and she's also smart and funny," Gabe said.

"Oh no, our comrade has fallen again," Billy said poking fun at Gabe.

Gabe took a long swig of his cold beer, "I'll admit there's something about her…"

"Why settle down when you have the whole female population falling at your feet?" Billy asked.

"I'm a one-woman kind of guy, despite how it might appear sometimes," he said.

They all guffawed at that statement.

"You could have fooled me," Derek teased.

"Hey so I've been playing the field since Sydney and I broke up…I wasn't ready to date anyone seriously, but now, with Annie… she could make a man change his mind in a heartbeat," he said staring off into space.

"Earth to Gabe, where in the hell did you go man?" Rocker, the drummer in the band said, snapping his fingers in front of Gabe's face.

"La la land…or should I say the land of Annie," Billy responded.

"Give the guy a break, he obviously has it bad," Derek defended his friend.

"Alright let's hit the road; we have a bit of a drive ahead of us, the life of a musician," Gabe grinned.

"Yeah, we have it sooo rough," Rocker added. As if to prove his point one of the female bartenders approached with a flirtatious smile and handed him her phone number jotted down on a napkin.

"Call me next time you play in the area. I could put you all up at my place," she offered.

"We might take you up on that, Kylie," Rocker said.

"You do that, bye now," she said walking away.

"Now who is in La la land?" Gabe poked back.

CHAPTER 5

The following morning Annie slept in until ten and was the last to get up.

Linda was alone and, as promised, curled up with a book on the back-deck lounge chair, sipping a glass of orange juice.

"Where is everybody?" Annie asked.

"They went into town for some pastries. Abbey heard there was a fabulous French bakery. They should be back any minute. The coffee is already made. How is your head this morning?" she said grinning.

"A little foggy, but all things considered, not too bad," Annie said.

"Things got a little frisky with the cowboy last night, do tell," Linda pried.

"I'm so embarrassed, I think I came on a little too strong." she confided.

"Nonsense, this is the twenty-first century; give yourself a break. I'm sure he's used to it anyway. Being in a band and all that, kind of goes with the territory," Linda replied.

"Yeah, that's what scares me, what woman in their right mind would want to deal with that all the time?" she replied to her friend.

"A beautiful, confident woman, who knows herself, and what she wants... I happen to know a woman like that..." Linda said, tongue in cheek.

"I'm not that secure—it may appear so on the outside, but underneath, I'm as insecure as the next person."

"He might be worth the effort; I mean the way he jumped down from the stage to rescue you last night...I mean come on!" Linda said holding her hand over her heart for emphasis.

Blushing slightly, Annie said, "He would have done that for anyone in the same position."

"Something tells me you brought out the alpha male in him, but sure... whatever you say," she drawled sarcastically.

The door banged open and the girls whirled in carrying two large white pastry boxes and wearing satisfied grins.

"Scored," Zoey crowed.

"Cream horns," Abbey said, rolling her eyes up in dramatized ecstasy. "Fresh, made right there, flakey crust, glorious cream, I can't wait another moment," she said, filling a mug with coffee.

They all gathered around the boxes, grabbing their choice of delectable goodies as if they were starving. Zoey took a moment to size up Annie. "How are you feeling boss?"

"Not bad," she responded.

"How were your dreams last night?" she said teasing her friend.

"Pretty steamy," she retorted.

"I'll bet they were," she nodded approvingly.

"I'd be jumping on that one if I were you. Men like that don't grow on trees around here," she said.

"Stop. I'm not ready to have a man in my life, other than J.J. and my future brother-in-law," she said.

"We don't always have control over every little thing, sometimes fate has a way of stepping in," Zoey counseled.

They all sat in a circle, enjoying their sweet pastries and staring at Annie, who took one last large bite of her cream horn, finishing it with relish. "Now, enough about my love life, what are the plans for the day?"

"We're still going kayaking; did you change your mind and decide to join us?"

"Yes, I made a promise to myself that there would be more play in my life and dammit I'm going to keep that promise." Annie declared.

~

*P*addling away from shore, Annie let the sun, wind, and water literally and figuratively carry her away. She leaned back for a moment, closed her eyes, and let the rays of the sun warm her cheeks. She had thrown on an old navy tank top, khaki cargo shorts, and her trusty waterproof Teva sandals. Her hair was tied back in a ponytail. She loved the sound of the waves lapping at the hull of her sea kayak. The water was calm today and her vessel, built for stability not speed, would be able to handle any choppy waters they might encounter on their voyage. The sounds of the shore birds were ancient and gave Annie a sense of being in another place in time.

They had all slathered on the sunscreen and had packed some fruit and snacks and plenty of water. Nothing to do, nowhere to be but in the present. They were quiet and contemplative, enjoying this opportunity to be out in nature and on the water. Following the shoreline for direction, their destination was a cove they had been told about along this route. Once they reached the inlet, they planned to get out and stretch, take a break and eat their snacks.

Annie dipped her paddle back in the water and began to gently row, enjoying the feel of her muscles engaged with the resistance of the water. The breeze tempered the heat from the sun and kept her cool as she began to exert more effort in moving forward.

"Look." Abbey squealed pointing up at the sky. "That's a bald eagle," she said excitedly.

"Oh my God. You're right," Annie replied. She had seen a bald eagle on the trail ride with Gabe, and she couldn't help but wonder whether it was a mysterious sign of some kind or simply a coincidence. She felt a quiver of excitement in her belly thinking about it. The stirring in her soul, almost a yearning, made her feel vulnerable but not in an entirely unpleasant way.

Ahead they could see the cliffs and where the shoreline disappeared, a little more paddling and they would arrive at the inlet. Zoey and Madison were the first to disembark from their kayaks. The small sandy cove was surrounded by steep cliffs and it was breathtakingly beautiful. A perfect place to rest and enjoy their snacks.

Since the first two had already pulled their kayaks to shore, they helped Abbey and Annie stabilize their boats so they could hop out and pull them to land, lining them up with the other bright colored boats.

"I want to live here," Madison said.

"I know, me too," Abbey agreed.

"I wish the others had come along, they are really missing out on something special," Zoey said.

"I know, but sometimes you need to chill," Annie said.

"Truth," Zoey concurred.

They all munched on their snacks, silent now, taking in the beauty of their surroundings. Annie had taken off her sandals and snuggled her toes and fingers into the warm sand, enjoying the sensuous feel of letting the granules sift through her fingers. Leaning back, she stretched her long shapely legs out in front of her and leaned on her elbows for support.

"Sometimes I wonder what it was like to live a hundred years ago, no cell phones, and before everyone owned an automobile. Can you imagine? I know technology has made our lives easier in many ways, but I wonder at what price?" she mused.

"Yeah, I'll take the modern any day of the week. Can you imagine having to hand wash your clothes in a stream, wringing them out, and hanging them to dry?" Zoey said.

"I know, everyone worked hard, but they had to use their imaginations and creativity for entertainment. Music, singing, games, talking, playing outdoors… it seems so peaceful…" Annie said wistfully.

"You can unplug, you know. Set a day aside and turn off all your electronics. No phone, TV, or internet, it's amazing how hard it is but also how liberating at the same time." Abbey said.

"I'm going to do more of that, this place brings me back to something deep inside of myself, a longing for..."

She was interrupted by Zoey exclaiming, "A cowboy."

They all burst out laughing, Annie blushing at the hint of truth in her friend's joke. She would keep that to herself though. She wasn't ready to examine the feelings that her encounter with Gabe had aroused inside of her.

Annie jumped up, suddenly restless, and walked to the water's edge, wading in up to her knees. It was still too cold to swim but the sun kissing her skin kept the chill at bay. The breeze ruffled wisps of unruly hair that had been freed from the confines of the elastic band. So deep in thought was she that a gull's shriek startled her out of her reverie, and she laughed out loud in surprise.

"Girls, what do you think? Should we head back?" Annie asked.

"Yes, I'm ready," Zoey replied.

The sun and the water had worked their magic, and everyone was relaxed and content.

CHAPTER 6

*G*abe rubbed his hands across his face and raked his fingers through his scalp, further tousling the already unruly mop of hair as he reread a letter with contractual forms attached, he'd received that afternoon. It was an inquiry about his availability to take on a young horse with some behavioral issues due to an early trauma.

The thing that had Gabe scratching his head was that this particular request had come from the owner of a prestigious horse farm in Lexington Kentucky, Imperial Farms, one known for breeding the most elite show horses in the competitive equestrian group of hunter jumpers. Some of their horses fetched up to a million plus in sales. A score like this would certainly be a big boost for his training credentials and portfolio.

He was curious to know if this could be a referral from Tucker Noll farms, since he had managed to work miracles on one of their champion mares several years ago. Since Tucker was also from Lexington, that made the most sense. Word did seem to travel in the horse world, reputations could be made or broken in an instant.

The timing wasn't the best since Sam was currently away for a month. Gabe was not only responsible for his own duties as manager of the farm and horse trainer on his own time, but he was picking up the slack that Sam's absence caused. He wished Sam were here to bounce things off. *I'll make it work.*

"I'm done mucking the stalls, got something else fer me to do?" Gabe was startled out of his musings by Slim, who now stood at the office door fidgeting with his cowboy hat.

Five-foot-six-inches of wiry muscle, scruff, and grit. He was gruff in manner with a sarcastic edge, and it didn't take more than a few minutes talking with him to understand that this guy had been around the proverbial block a time or two and had the cynicism to prove it.

He had started working there the previous fall, when he had answered their ad in a monthly horse journal. Slim had over forty years' experience in the equine industry. He was worth his weight in gold as far as Gabe was concerned. A hard worker, albeit a little rough around the edges, he had a way with the horses; in fact, he was much better with animals then he was with people. Gabe had grown to depend on him, maybe not for sitting around bullshitting, but for keeping things running smoothly around the farm.

"Did you check on Whiskey?" Gabe asked. Sam's horse had recently come up lame from a hoof abscess.

"He's prit near sound. I soaked his hoof again this mornin and hand-walked him around a bit. Darn if he hain't puttin full weight on that leg and I could hardly pick up on a limp."

"That's great news Slim. Go ahead and call it a day. Tomorrow we'll get started on baling hay while we have the dry weather for it. Looks like this whole week will be perfect balin' weather," Gabe said. "I've got a couple of young guys lined up to help, so we should be good for labor. Slim I'm putting you in charge but go easy on them." He grinned to soften his directive.

"If they do their dang dern jobs I won't have to go hard," he griped. "The group you hired in the fall were useless."

"Now Slim, you were young once… they're learning. Think of yourself as their teacher instead of their boss. That'll take ya a whole lot further than yelling will," Gabe said.

He could tell his advice was going in one ear and out the other. Shaking his head in disgust, Slim plunked his old worn out cowboy hat back onto his balding crown and shuffled out the door. Gabe listened to Slim grumble under his breath as he left, amused at how prickly the old cowboy could be.

Gabe returned to the problem at hand and decided to consult with Zane Dunn about taking on this latest equine client. Zane was a sharp attorney and it would ease his mind to talk with him about the liabilities and legalities of the contract. He wanted to make sure to cover his ass, because he certainly couldn't afford to pay them back for a million-dollar horse if something bad were to happen to it.

He had to admit to himself that not only did he feel flattered, but he felt an inner excitement at the prospect of working with the troubled filly. The thought that he could potentially reach a very large audience appealed to his altruistic nature. He knew he had a calling to help as many horses as he could, and that started with educating the folks in the horse world about the essence of horses and working with their nature rather than against it.

He had dreams of obliterating the cruel practices and the old ways of "breaking" a horse and of being a part of the evolution of a new paradigm. This seemed like a golden opportunity to do that.

Gabe knew that the best way to clear his head was to hop on the back of his horse, so he strode toward the barn to saddle up his palomino Gil. Gil and he had a bond that cowboys dream of. There was a mutual trust and respect that had saved Gabe's ass many a time out on the trail.

Everything dropped away when they were out in nature together, and the two became one. They communicated almost telepathically, Gabe would think left and Gil would move left. So complete was his trust, Gabe thought that Gil would walk through fire for him, as Gabe certainly would for Gil.

He grabbed his halter and lead from the tack room and went to fetch Gil. When he arrived at the pasture gate, he let out a loud whistle and, hearing the familiar sound, Gil came thundering in from the field, whinnying a greeting as he galloped toward Gabe.

"Hey big fella, how is my best bud today?" he said offering him an oat treat. Gil took the proffered treat with his soft lips searching Gabe's outstretched palm, warm breath blowing through his nostrils. Slipping the halter on, he walked him back to the barn to tack up

He had decided at the last minute to ride bareback

which he preferred, loving the tighter communication that the closer contact provided. There was something sacred about sitting on a thousand-plus pound animal, one that you really could never take the "wild" out of, that was not only a privilege, but humbling. To feel the strength and muscle under your seat, to feel every movement as they, in turn, felt yours, was satisfying on a deep level.

Gabe hopped on and they headed toward the wooded trail that he and Sam painstakingly kept clear of invasive honeysuckle and fallen tree branches and the occasional tree. He let Gil have his head and they meandered at a slow pace, neither in any hurry, nowhere else to be. The trees were leafed out, shading the path as they followed the twists and turns through hills and dales. They weren't too far along when Gabe heard a cry coming from the brush alongside the trail. "Whoa," he said as he jumped down from Gil to peer into the thick tangle of vines, branches, and greenery.

He softly called out, "Here Kitty, here kitty." Suddenly a small kitten sprang from the thicket, mewing frantically to convey it's panic at the predicament he was in.

"Aww, you're a cute little fella," he said picking up the small orange kitten, holding him up to check and confirm the gender. "I guess we could use another barn cat. Now how in the world did you get all the way out here?" he said in a soothing voice. The terrified kitten, knowing he was now safe, transformed and began loudly purring.

Gabe walked around to show Gil the tiny bundle he held, and Gil nuzzled the soft orange ball of fluff, his breath ruffling its fur. "I guess this means our ride is going to be cut a little short... oh well, that's the way it goes sometimes." He tucked the kitten inside his tee shirt then hopped back on his mount for the return ride to the farm.

He passed Slim's trailer home as Slim was taking one last puff of his cigarette. He stubbed it out in the coffee can he kept on his front stoop.

"When ya going to give up that nasty habit?" Gabe said.

"That'd be never," Slim replied. He never smoked while at work, and never at the barn. Smoking and barns were a recipe for disaster and Gabe had a firm rule about it, but he figured what his employees did on their own time was none of his business.

"Hey look what found us on our ride?" he said pulling out the kitten for Slim to see. "I think you could use a companion," he said, only half joking.

"I'll be a horse's bee-hind, I had an orange cat years ago, Rotten was his name, he was my favorite cat, he lived for almost 20 years. I cried like a baby when that durned old cat died. Here hand him to me," he commanded reaching up for the small kitten. "I reckon he hain't no more'n six or seven weeks. Let ol' Slim getcha some food and water." The normally crotchety man was suddenly talking baby talk much to Gabe's amusement.

"That was easier than I expected," Gabe said.

"I may be an old salty bastard, but I still got a soft spot for critters. It's the dang blame humans that get under my skin," he admitted.

"You're as tough as old shoe leather, but I always suspected that your heart was mushy underneath that exterior." Gabe enjoyed having a real conversation with Slim. They were far and few between.

"Don't get used to it, it's reserved for animals only... the four-legged kind, unless they've lost a limb, then the three-leggeds have my blessin' as well," he said, letting the slightest of grins turn up his lip.

"Help yourself to the dry food up at the barn, I'm sure he's pretty hungry," Gabe offered.

"I'll do that until I kin git to the store and pick up some kitten chow. What do ya think little feller?" Slim said, continuing with his baby talk. "I think I'll name him Gus, after my Pa."

"I'll leave you to it then, I've got some office business to finish up with," Gabe said. "By the way, you don't happen to know of anyone worth hiring to help out around here do ya? I'm thinking maybe twenty-five to thirty hours a week?"

"Naw, I don't know nobody, but there was a young guy wanderin around here yesterday asking for the owner or manager, he mighta been looking fer some work," Slim said. "I tole him you weren't around, so he might be back."

"Send him my way if he shows up again, I'll be in the office for the next couple of hours catching up on some paperwork," Gabe said. Slim turned his back to Gabe and entered the trailer, letting the screen door slam shut behind him.

Shaking his head at Slim's abrupt departure, he rode back to the barn. After a quick brush and several treats, he watched Gill gallop to join the rest of the herd. Returning to the tack room, which also served as an office, he put on a pot of coffee and sat at his desk.

Without consciously knowing it, sometime during his short ride he had decided to submit his resume and accept the offer to work with this troubled filly, unless Zane advised against it. It was an offer he couldn't refuse. It had the potential to shoot him to the top of the list of trainers and that would be a dream come true for Gabe.

CHAPTER 7

With the bachelorette weekend behind her, Annie's life was back to status quo, meaning working her butt off at the salon. Taking a Saturday off for the lakeside retreat had set her schedule back, and she had added extra appointments in to accommodate her clients. It did make the time fly; it was already Thursday.

A week from Saturday, her friend would be tying the knot. *Another one bites the dust.* Everyone else had already left for the day and she sat at the front counter in a slight daze from fatigue. She knew she needed to get home to the dogs, but she couldn't rouse herself to move at that moment.

She was startled out of her trance by a movement at the front window of the salon. She remembered that she had locked the door behind Zoey when she had left, but she still jumped slightly when she saw a face peering in at her. It only took a moment for her to realize who it was, and her fear quickly turned into annoyance.

He was aware the second she noticed him, and he waved a large bouquet of roses at her through the front window while wearing his most charming expression. Pantomiming for her to unlock the door and let him in, she shook her head no. Annie picked up the phone and pretended to be talking into the receiver smiling at Bradley and shrugging as if to say, 'sorry busy with work what can I do?'

He held up the flowers and again motioned for her to open the door. By this time Annie had convinced herself she was being silly and paranoid—after all this was Bradley, a cop, her ex-lover, someone she had loved and spent several years with. What was wrong with her? She was starting to let everyone's opinion get to her. She knew him and knew he wouldn't hurt her. She walked over to the door and unlocked it for him, and he quickly entered and thrust the flowers toward her.

"Hey Annie."

She reluctantly took the roses from him. "Bradley, I can't accept these. You must stop. It's over." she said.

Bradly ignored her and continued, "I have been really worried about you. You haven't been home in almost a week."

"Are you following me? That is not okay. Do you understand me?" Annie said.

"No, I am not "following" you, I drove by your townhouse several times on my patrol duty and noticed that your car hasn't been there. Don't get paranoid on me."

"I threw a bachelorette party for Abbey at the lake last weekend, so I was away," she said, not elaborating about her house-sitting gig for Darcy.

"Annie, I'm lost without you. I need to feel you in my

arms again," he said. He grabbed Annie's arm and pulled her into his embrace. He hugged her tightly to his chest while nuzzling her neck. The flowers were crushed as she tried to wedge her hands against his chest to push against him.

"Bradley, let me go!" she said.

"One kiss, please," he said while capturing her chin and forcing his lips against hers.

"I said *no!*" Annie yelled as she pushed with all her might and was finally able to escape from his clutches. "Get out now." she commanded. "*Now!*" Annie pointed at the door. Glancing down at the flowers which were now a pile of scattered petals and broken stems at her feet, she felt a chill go up her spine.

"Annie, what's gotten into you? This is all your sister. I can hear her voice. This isn't you... I know you better," he said.

"O-U-T!" She replied threateningly.

"Okay, I'm out of here. Wow Annie you have really changed, and not for the better," he said.

"It is long overdue" she replied firmly, locking the door behind him.

～

After waiting a half hour, Annie left the salon, heading home to Darcy's place. She vigilantly watched for any signs that she was being followed and was convinced that she hadn't been. After deactivating the alarm, she crouched down to greet Freddie, Fannie, and Mac, her three roommates.

They were all twists and wiggles as they exuberantly welcomed their aunt. She let them outside and then went directly to Darcy's bedroom to see if her sister kept a gun in the bedside drawer. This act alone proved she was more rattled than she had realized, because she loathed guns.

She gave a sigh of relief upon finding that it was still there. Darcy had taken her out to a firing range several times in the past, but she still couldn't hit the broad side of a barn. Yet knowing that she at least knew how to use it, if she had to, gave her some comfort. She only prayed that she would never have to.

As she fed the dogs her cell phone rang. Annie let it go to voicemail. She would check it later. The canines gobbled their dinner in record time and Annie, who had stuck a frozen pizza in the oven for herself, dug in. Throwing some pieces of crust to her attentive audience made her laugh out loud as their unblinking eyes watched her every move.

"Okay guys let's go outside one more time and then curl up together and watch some TV," she said.

Twenty minutes later they were all piled up on the sectional couch to watch reruns of *The Gilmore Girls.* She had slipped into her PJs, an oversized tee shirt and patterned cotton boxer shorts. She stretched her long legs out in front of her and propped several pillows behind her head. Fannie nestled in next to her and rested her head on Annie's lap to stare up at her with her big brown eyes.

"Your Mama will be home before you know it girl," she said. She could tell they were a bit confused by Annie now sitting where Darcy normally sat. Fannie wagged her tail as if she understood what Annie was telling her then closed her eyes and was soon fast asleep.

As she switched off the bedside lamp around midnight, she remembered that she hadn't checked her voice mail but decided it could wait until the morning. She fell into a troubled sleep, with dreams of danger lurking in the dark shadows.

～

The bright sunlight entering through the bedroom window aroused her from sleep. Glancing at the bedside clock she saw it was already seven thirty. She hurriedly jumped out of bed with the dogs dancing around her heels. After letting them out she put on a pot of coffee. Remembering her voicemail, she played the message from the night before and her heart literally skipped a beat.

"Hey Annie, it's me Gabe," he said, as if she could forget that sexy voice, "I was hoping I could see you this weekend, maybe go out for a drink and a bite to eat? Give me a call."

She had to sit down, so she plopped on the stool closest to her, more excited than she wanted to admit.

"Oh my God!" she said out loud. After not hearing from him right away she had assumed he wasn't interested and she had let it go...but now, what the hell. She couldn't contain the huge smile that lit up her face. She felt excited and noticed a very tingly response between her thighs at the sound of his voice. He was such a guy, and a beautiful one at that. She hoped she was a match for him but by God she couldn't say no even if her better senses told her to do so.

He answered on the first ring, "Hey Gabe, it's me, Annie."

"Annie." Somehow the way he said her name made it sound like a caress.

"Hi…" she said shyly.

"I really want to see you again; would you be interested in going out me with tomorrow night?" he asked.

"Yes, I'd like that."

"Good. Do you like barbeque?"

"I love good barbeque," she said.

"I have a place in mind. It's about an hour away, casual, then we can come back to town and go out for a beer, sound good to you?" he asked.

"Yes. I'm really looking forward to it."

"Text me your address and I'll pick you up around six thirty if that works for you."

"Perfect, I work until five—that will give me time to take care of the dogs and get ready," she said.

"See you then, Annie." His voice was soft and husky.

"Yes, see you then," she replied. She clutched the phone tightly while pressing her other hand against her racing heart. After disconnecting, she danced light-heartedly around the room, pirouetting with perfect balance and grace, her cheeks flushed with exhilaration. She hoped she could get through today and tomorrow without exploding.

"OK Annie, get your butt moving…you now have thirty minutes to shower, get out that door, into your car and drive to the salon," she scolded herself. With that she floated forward into her day, somewhere far above her ordinary existence, and managed to arrive at the salon before her first client.

~

"*Y*ou are in an awfully good mood today Ms. Morgan," James commented.

"Oh really? How can you tell?"

"Spill it. I know you so well. It has to be that cowboy everyone was talking about… the guy in the band that jumped off the stage to rescue the damsel in distress," he teased.

Annie stuck her tongue out at James and said, "I'm not talking, my lips are sealed."

"No fair," Zoey chimed in. "We are your best friends, what kind of friend keeps secrets from their besties?"

"Oh, it's nothing…a casual date tonight, dinner out, then we're going for a couple of drinks afterwards," Annie finally confessed.

"I can't stand it. This is so amazing, not to mention romantic. James this guy is so *hot*!" Zoey said, fanning herself.

"So is our Annie," James said. "No one is good enough for our beautiful girl."

"It is a date everyone. No big deal. That is why I wasn't going to tell y'all I knew you would make a production out of it," Annie said.

"I'm just sayin' you are lit up from the inside and you may be fooling yourself, but I have not seen you look this wound up for a very long time," Zoey pointed out.

"I'm nervous as all git-out. I haven't been out on a first date in over four years," Annie admitted.

"You will be fine darlin'. I can't help myself… I have to say it…save a horse, ride a cowboy," then James began laughing hysterically at his own joke referencing a line from a country song. She and Zoey couldn't help but join in, not because the joke was so funny, but because James was getting such a kick out of it.

"I may have to do that." Annie responded after their laughter had subsided.

"You go girl," James said. "Giddy up," he said, then more laughter ensued.

"You are terrible J.J., I can't tell you anything," Annie said. She pretended to be annoyed.

"You know you love me," he replied. "I love you too by the way. I've lived vicariously through you my dear—after fifteen years with the same partner, there isn't much new to talk about," he said, belying the truth that he was completely content and still madly in love with William.

"We are all jealous of you and you know it," Annie said. "We all wish for a love like yours."

"Mark my words, you will have it, there is not a doubt in my mind," he declared.

"I hope you are right, but for now I am happily single."

"Not for long," he said, grinning from ear to ear.

"Stop it. I mean it." She was embarrassed at the scrutiny of her dating life before it had even started.

"Okay I'll lay off for now. Go and have a good time."

"I plan on it, thanks." She was relieved to finally move away from that subject matter as her first customer walked through the door.

CHAPTER 8

"Oh, why did I agree to this," Annie said, talking to the dogs who were watching her as she paced the hardwood floors waiting for the knock at the door. "I must have been out if my mind." Suddenly the dogs began barking, which could only mean one thing…

Annie opened the door as Gabe held up his fist to knock. Surprised to see her standing there, he quickly recovered and handed her a bunch of daisies with the stems wrapped in soggy paper towels and a baggie secured with an elastic band to keep them fresh.

"Thank you, Gabe," Annie said. Taking the offering from his strong tanned hands she said, "I'll put them in water. Please come in; don't mind the three canines, they are very friendly." He stooped to their level to greet them.

"Nice place," he said, looking around from his crouched postion.

"It's not mine, it's Darcy's place. I'm housesitting for her," she explained.

"Not a bad gig."

"I'm not complaining."

Gabe was dressed casually in faded blue jeans and a tucked-in gray Bob Seger concert tee-shirt. He wore his old worn brown leather cowboy boots, which were a big turn-on. She almost laughed out loud thinking of James' joke yesterday. Yes indeed, riding a cowboy was becoming more appealing by the minute. He looked as fine as anything she had ever laid eyes on. The laugh lines around his light brown eyes told their own story, and they sparkled as if he was in on a joke nobody else was aware of.

Annie had decided to keep it simple herself, choosing a black cotton spaghetti-strap jump suit which showed off her slim honey-toned arms and curvy figure. She had slipped on a pair of open-toed sandals, which exposed Rachel's handiwork, a pedicure with brightly painted pink toenails. Throwing the dogs their treats, she stepped out into the beautiful spring evening, anticipation tingling her senses.

Gabe felt aroused at the sight of her. The swell of her breasts through the soft cotton fabric, with a hint of cleavage, made Gabe long to see more. Her red hair was held away from her face by two combs, leaving it to cascade down her back in thick waves. He wanted to pull the clips from her hair and see her naked flesh writhing with desire for him.

Pressing his hand into the small of her back, he led her to the passenger side of his old blue pickup truck where he opened the door for her. His hungry eyes lingered on her creamy skin as she climbed in. Gabe closed the door and jogged around to jump behind the wheel.

He turned in his seat to face her, "Annie…" His eyes glittered with heat.

"Gabe." She looked down because she suddenly felt too exposed and vulnerable.

"You are so beautiful; do you know that?" he asked.

"Thank you."

"Annie, I don't want to scare you off, but I'm seriously into you. I honestly don't think I have ever been this attracted to a woman in my entire life. It's put me at a severe disadvantage."

She smiled at him exposing her dimples, then said, "Tell me more, I kind of like the sound of that."

He reached over and stroked his thumb across her full lips, causing her to suddenly feel wet between her thighs. Her large green eyes grew wide when he slipped his hand all the way down her bare arm to clasp her hand. He rubbed the tender spot in her palm, then he brought it to his lips and planted a kiss in the center, which felt directly linked to her womanhood. She inhaled sharply as his tongue darted out to tantalize her further. His warm eyes danced with humor as they met hers, knowing full well the effect he was having on her nervous system. She found herself mesmerized by his seductive powers and helpless to do anything about it.

"Oh Annie, you have no idea…" She stared at him as if in a trance, which wasn't too far off the mark. "Stop looking at me like that or we will never make it to the barbeque joint," he said, effectively breaking the spell.

"Sorry," she said.

"For what? Making me crazy with desire for you? That's not your fault, Annie girl," he said, tweaking her nose as he turned and started the truck.

So electrified was the energy between them that

Annie felt like crawling out of her skin with longing. It was only after Gabe turned on the radio and began singing along softly that she began to unwind a little.

"Our band does this cover," Gabe said, referring to the song playing, *Let Me Down Easy*, by Billy Currington.

"I love this song!" Annie said.

"I knew you were a country girl at heart."

"So now you know, the secret is out."

"I could have written this song for you, it pretty much says it all, I am barely hangin' on." Stealing a line from the song, he said, "If I fall will you let me down easy?" He continued singing along with the romantic song, lyrics about being on the edge of falling, leaving his heart with her, her scent, tasting her kiss...glancing over at Annie, and seeing her eyes sparkling with desire, Gabe suddenly became tongue tied. Her incredible beauty and her complete lack of awareness of it, made her even more stunning if that was possible.

"Your eyes, damn Annie, a guy like me could get completely lost in that sea of green," he confessed.

She looked down at her lap then glanced back up to meet his burning gaze. She knew she was in big trouble, teetering on the edge of a cliff, diving, free falling, tumbling down to God only knew where.

"Gabe... I don't know what to say, I mean, this is intense, I am a bit overwhelmed," she said, while wringing her hands.

"Hey, I didn't mean to throw you Annie, let's go with the flow and enjoy where we're at and if it's meant to be it will be. Deal?"

"Deal," she said. The electricity in the truck practically bounced off the cab. She dazzled him with her smile. He reached for her hand and held it for the rest of the way.

They arrived at the barbeque restaurant and the first thing she noticed was the giant pig floating in the air over the building. Next, she saw that the parking lot was full and there was a line outside waiting to be seated. They put their names on the list and stood outside to wait.

"It must be pretty good food to attract a crowd like this," Annie commented.

"You have no idea. It is the best southern barbeque you will find north of the Carolinas."

"I'm starving, how about you?" she said. It was innocent enough until his gaze scorched her lips.

"Oh yeah, I am definitely starving..." He smiled, trying to lighten the intensity but failing to do so, put his arms around her waist and pulled her against him. She rested her hands on his chest and looked up at him, her eyes glowing with desire. As he leaned down for a kiss, they heard Gabe's name called, informing them that their table was ready.

Gabe said, "I could take you right here, right now, on this patio, I want you so bad."

"Down boy," Annie said.

"Too late for that."

Annie laughed and grabbed his hand, practically dragging him along behind her and into the restaurant. They were immediately seated at a booth in the middle of the noisy eatery. There was a fun, casual vibe with lots of conversation and laughter all around them. Strangely the raucous crowd almost provided a sense of privacy and anonymity.

Annie studied the menu intently as Gabe studied her. He couldn't help himself. He felt like he could get lost with her, go completely off the grid for the rest of his life, and never grow tired of being in her presence.

He couldn't quite figure it out. He had been with many beautiful women over the years, he had even loved a couple of them, but this felt unlike anything he had ever experienced before. Annie was the whole package...authentic, warm, smart, funny, sexy as hell, and the most exquisite creature he had ever laid eyes on.

Glancing up, Annie was startled to catch Gabe's fixed stare. His eyes practically glittered, the golden flecks standing out even more.

"Have you even looked at the menu?" Annie asked.

"I don't have to and besides, I like what I'm looking at right now," he replied.

"I'm getting the pulled chicken barbeque sandwich with their slaw as a side," she said.

"I always get the same thing, a rack of ribs, slow cooked collard greens, and their crispy corn fritters, which I'll happily share with you," he said.

The waitress arrived with their drinks, then took their food order, leaving them alone again.

"Not to sound cliché, but tell me about yourself," Gabe said.

"Ask me a question," Annie responded.

"How did you end up owning a salon? Had it always been a dream of yours?"

"Yes and no," she said. "I was always a girlie girl, I loved make-up, costumes, dresses, dolls. I could play for hours by myself, dressing my dolls in fancy clothes, doing their hair, completely the opposite of my sister Darcy, who was quite the tomboy and afraid of nothing.

Now don't get me wrong, my dolls could be quite adventurous," she said, then laughed at herself.

Gabe reached across the table to take Annie's hand in his, "Go on…"

"I hated high school, I hated classrooms, I hated studying, I was only there for the social interactions," she confessed. "I didn't have any desire to go to a university for the next four to six years of my life after graduating and I knew what I loved: art, horses and glamour," she said. "I didn't think I could find a way to support myself in the art world or the equine industry so that left me with my other passion, fashion, beauty, girlie stuff."

"Pretty sound logic," Gabe said.

"With my three sisters' support and encouragement, plus their financial backing I might add, I decided on a career in cosmetology, with the dream of owning and operating my own salon by the time I reached thirty," she said.

"I am pleased to say that I reached my goal ahead of schedule, and I now employ four stylists, two nail technicians, a licensed massage therapist, and an esthetician. Not too bad for someone who was such a terrible student."

"That is an amazing accomplishment Annie," he said. "University isn't for everyone, and it doesn't define a person's worth or intelligence. Some of the most educated people can be the dumbest and some folks that didn't even finish high school the smartest," he said.

"All I know is that university wasn't the right decision for me. I have never regretted it. I love my career, I love my colleagues, I love my life."

"Is there room in your life for one more thing to love?" he asked.

Annie caught her breath and said, "Part of my childhood dream always included marriage, children, a couple of dogs and horses...now, I don't know. I was really hurt in my last relationship, and I'm a little less idealistic than I used to be," she said.

"I would love to be the one to restore your faith," he said.

"How can you say that? You don't even know me, Gabe."

"I beg to differ, I can feel you, I can sense you, somehow I do know you," he insisted. "Call it intuition or a sixth sense, call it fate, a past life encounter, call it whatever you want, but I feel like I have known you forever."

"Oh Gabe, I feel like I'm being carried away on some big adventure and terrified that I'm not prepared for it. Your lifestyle, the band scene, music, women, I don't know if I can handle all of that."

"I am sorry if you feel overwhelmed, I can see how that all might be intimidating, but I don't mind taking the time to go slow, to show you that you don't have anything to worry about. Sometimes I forget that not everyone moves at my pace," he said.

"I am flattered, really I am, and it's not that I'm not wildly attracted to you, because I am. It's not that I don't think that you are kind and funny and crazy talented, because I do think that. It's about where I am in my life, just getting disentangled from a crazy relationship, I kind of lost confidence in myself. Let's take it slow...but not too slow," she smiled as she said the last part.

"All I ask for is a chance," he said, the relief he felt evident in his voice.

Their food arrived and they both dug in enthusiastically.

CHAPTER 9

After dinner they drove back to town and stopped at a dive bar Gabe frequented. They grabbed a table and Gabe went to order their beers. Handing Annie her bottle he said, "Are you still up for a game of pool?"

"Are you up for getting your butt kicked?"

"Ah, a little competitive I see."

"Just a tiny bit," Annie said.

"Let's see what you've got."

No one else was playing so they put their quarters in and Annie racked the balls.

"Should we flip to see who breaks?" she asked.

"Sure, I call heads." He pulled out a quarter and tossed it in the air, catching it to slap onto the back of his hand. He kept his palm covering it as he grinned at her, "Well what do you think it's going to be?"

"Tails of course," she grabbed at his hand trying to see who won.

"Drum roll please…" he slowly lifted his hand to

reveal the head of George Washington. "And he *scores!*" Gabe said, laughing at Annie's glare.

"Alright, tough guy, go ahead and shoot."

Gabe chalked up his cue stick and lined it up with the cue ball for his first shot. Annie watched his face, so serious in concentration, the way a stray lock of hair curled against his forehead, his sexy light stubble from skipping a shave, his broad shoulders and strong arms, even his hands were seductive. He pulled his elbow back and took his shot, the loud crack sending the balls flying in all directions with several going into the pockets.

"Not bad," Annie said. "You got two of each, which are you calling?"

"I'll call stripes," he said, after studying the table carefully.

He sank two more before a miscalculated bank shot cost him his turn.

Annie stepped up to the table and took aim, sinking three herself before missing. "I've got to go to the lady's room, I'll be right back," Annie said.

"Ready for another beer?"

"Sure."

Annie grabbed her clutch and went to find the restroom. It was about as big as a closet and the door didn't securely latch, but there was loads of graffiti in bathroom stalls and she loved reading it. She always had the urge to add something profound herself. Sometimes there were some really great poems and bits of wisdom alongside of the phone numbers and hearts with initials.

She washed her hands and pushed the dryer button which produced about enough air to move a speck of dust, maybe. Giving up she dried them on her pant legs and stepped back out.

As she looked around for Gabe, she saw that he was still standing at the bar in conversation with some hot brunette. She felt a pang of jealousy which she tamped down. Returning to the pool table she sat on a stool to wait. The girl was practically hanging on Gabe, flirting outrageously. Gabe didn't seem to mind, apparent as he stood there laughing at something she had just said.

He glanced over and saw Annie waiting and returned with their beers. "It's your turn," he said.

"Okay." She took aim, missing an easy shot.

"Woo hoo!" Gabe said, grinning.

When she didn't return his smile he said, "Is something wrong?"

"No."

"Are you sure, 'cause it sure seems like it."

"Just take your shot."

"Could this have anything to do with the girl I was just talking to?"

"Look Gabe, you don't owe me anything. It's not like we're in a committed relationship," she said.

"No, but I am on a date with you, and you're the only one that matters. She is just a fan of the band. That's all. It's part of the job. I don't even know her name."

"You don't need to explain," she said.

Gabe leaned his pool stick against the wall and pulled Annie into his arms.

"Apparently I do," he said as he lowered his head to kiss her. Lifting his lips but keeping them so close she could feel his breath he said, "You are all I think about. There is no one else. You've cast a spell on me."

"Really?" she said breathlessly.

"Really." He dipped his head again, burying his fingers in her thick hair as he took her mouth. He slid a hand down her back to pull her tighter against his pelvis. She could feel his hardness against her pubic bone. "Let's get out of here," he said.

"Let's," she agreed.

He looked deep into her eyes, the intensity stripping away any barriers she might have put between them. Taking her hand, he interlaced their fingers and led her out to the parking lot. Before opening the door, he backed her against the side of his truck and kissed her again. As he pressed against her she clung to him, wanting more.

"Gabe," she whispered against his lips.

"God Annie, what are you doing to me?"

He covered her mouth again and sensuously inserted his tongue inside her warmth and plundered. Their tongues danced until he captured hers and sucked on it gently. He reached for her breast and she gasped as he found her nipple and tugged on it through the thin fabric. Holding the weight in his hand he massaged and kneaded until her knees were weak. She clung to him, arms wrapped around his neck, not wanting their kiss to end.

He raised his head and let out a ragged breath, brushing his lips across hers one last time. "We'd better get on the road; it's getting late and if we don't rein it in now, we might pass the point of no return."

"The voice of reason. You're right of course. I need to get back to the dogs and it is almost midnight."

He opened the truck door and she climbed in. As he pulled his door shut, he looked at her and reached across to caress her face. "Know this, I don't really want to listen to that damn voice of reason, but I know it's steering me right."

"I agree. No reason to rush whatever this 'thing' is that we have."

"I don't want to rush it Annie—you're way too important to me."

They held hands the entire way home and Annie snuggled up against him with her head resting on his shoulder... Annie could barely keep her hands to herself. She had never desired a man so intensely as she did Gabe. Her very nerve fibers hummed with excitement.

"I feel like a schoolboy with a massive crush," Gabe admitted, confirming for Annie that he felt it too.

"I'm glad I'm not alone."

He pulled up the drive and left his truck running while he walked Annie to the door. They made another date for a trail ride the Sunday after her friend's wedding. She could hardly wait.

After letting the critters back in, she washed her face, flossed and brushed her teeth, then crawled into bed. Her phone pinged signaling a text message.

Gabe: Thank you for the best night of my life. I'll see you in my dreams, meet me by the Big Dipper in five...

Annie: Give me fifteen...Night

Smiling she turned off her lamp and snuggled into the soft down pillow.

CHAPTER 10

Gabe had finished turning out the herd and was heading to his office when Slim approached with a young man following closely behind.

"This here is the feller I was tellin' ya about the other day. He wants a job," Slim said.

Gabe studied the young man who appeared to be in his early twenties, strong and fit. "What brings you here to Parker Farms?" he asked.

"I recently moved to town and was asking around about job opportunities. I was raised around horses and was working for a horse ranch in Kentucky since I graduated from high school," he said.

"Come on into my office, we'll talk," Gabe said. "Do you have a resume on you?"

"No, not on me, but I have one. I can drop it by this afternoon if you think I have a shot at a job," he offered.

"I'd certainly have to see it before any formal decisions are made but if everything checks out, you're hired," Gabe said.

"That's great. I'll be happy to drop it off. By the way, I'm Cal, Cal Smith, pleased to meet you," he said, smiling warmly.

"I'm Gabe Hunter, I manage the place, and I train and give a few lessons here and there in my free time. What brings you all the way to Michigan from Kentucky?"

"I'm a little embarrassed to say, but I met a girl on the internet, we fell in love and now I'm here," he said.

"Romance in the twenty-first century," Gabe said, grinning.

"Yeah, I guess that's about right," he agreed.

"It sounds like you have the experience I'm looking for. I'm offering 25 to 30 hours per week, sometimes a little more, I'll pay $16 an hour starting out and raise it to $17 after the first six months. I'll need you to work weekends sometimes. Will that be a problem?" he asked.

"Not at all. I'm happy to have the opportunity to work for you. You are quite the accomplished trainer, according to some of the locals I've talked to. It appears you have a reputation as being somewhat of a horse whisperer," he shared.

"Don't believe everything you hear," Gabe said, grinning. "When can you start?"

"Tomorrow," he replied.

"Drop off your resume and your contact info and I'll look it over and get back with you this evening."

"Wow that's great! Thank you, Mr. Hunter." Cal said. "You won't regret this."

"Call me Gabe please, we're all one big happy family here. The owner, Sam Parker, is away for the month, but he is a great guy and my best friend, he's easy to get along with."

"What's with the guy that introduced us?" Cal asked.

"That's Slim, hardworking, honest as the day is long, and gets on better with the animals than people, his bark is worse than his bite," Gabe said.

"If you say so, I don't think he was very impressed with me," Cal said.

"That's his way, don't waste your energy worrying about it, as long as you work hard and do the job you were hired to do, you'll get along fine," he said. "Remember, Slim does have seniority, so what he says goes. But on the other hand, if there are problems, you report them to me."

"Yes sir," Cal responded.

"Glad you stopped by, and if everything checks out, I'd like you to start tomorrow, six a.m. We're baling hay and we'll need all the help we can get."

"I'll be here." he said smiling from ear to ear.

Walking around the barn whistling, Gabe couldn't believe his good luck. What timing. What were the odds that the perfect farm hand would show up when he needed him the most?

The only blip had been when Slim had approached him after Cal had left, to tell him that he didn't like the kid. He said he couldn't put his finger on it he just didn't trust him. Seeing as Slim didn't like anyone, Gabe chose to ignore his judgement and trust his own instincts.

The kid seemed likeable enough, and he showed enthusiasm. It also didn't hurt that he was built like a welter weight champion, solid muscle. Why, if Slim were smart, he would welcome him with open arms. He should be happy to have some young muscle around the place to relieve him of some of the heavier duties around the farm.

This latest turn of events was the green light Gabe needed to feel good about his decision to take on the filly from Imperial Farms… if he got the chance. It seemed like everything was giving him the go-ahead. Zane had looked over the paperwork and felt it was pretty cut and dried, encouraging Gabe to move forward. He would make the call today and proceed with the application process.

~

As he was going over Cal's references later that day, Pepper, who had recently started boarding her horse there, popped her head through the door to say hello.

"Hi Gabe, I thought I'd check in to see how you are holding up with Sam gone," she said.

"Hanging in there. Speaking of … FYI, there is going to be a new face running around the farm. His name is Cal. You'll recognize him, he's the young, strong, good-looking one, with blond hair and blue eyes. I'm sure that will be a nice change of scenery after looking at Slim and me every day," he said.

"You two hotties would be hard to beat. Seriously, I know it'll be a relief for you guys to have some more help around here. I don't know how you do it all," she said.

"I love every minute of it, that's how I do it," Gabe replied.

"Even so, I'll bet you'll be glad to see Sam again."

"You got that right. I'm also adding another client to

my training roster. It's a big-deal horse from a prestigious Kentucky horse farm, and it could be the platform I need to help me launch my reputation as a specialized trainer," he said unable to disguise his excitement.

"That is great Gabe. You deserve it more than anyone I know," she said sincerely. "Speaking of deserving…Have you been in the recording studio lately? Last time we talked, you and your band were working on a new CD of your original songs."

"Yeah, that's kinda on the back burner right now, and this latest horse project will probably push it even further back," Gabe said.

"Oh, to be so talented that you have to choose which passion to follow must be really rough," Pepper said.

"It might sound good, but choices like that can be tough. Feels like there isn't enough of me to go around and letting go of something you love, even if it's to move toward something equally good, sucks. Fortunately, I mostly get to have my cake and eat it too."

"I love your band, you guys are all very talented musicians and I think you could really make it…you'd probably have a better chance in Nashville though—*God* don't tell Sam I said that, he would kill me for even suggesting it!"

"Thanks for the vote of confidence Pepper, and your secret is safe with me."

"I speak the truth," she replied, tucking a strand of her recently-shorn brown hair behind her ear. "I have to get going, I'm working the graveyard shift at the hospital tonight, and I wanted to get a quick ride in this afternoon."

"Good luck getting him in from the field today. That

green grass is like candy after the long winter we had," he said laughing.

"I'm armed with the real thing," she said, showing him a peppermint candy.

"Ha, that should do it," he said.

"See ya, around Gabe."

"Yep," he replied, returning to his perusal of Cal's resume.

He really liked Pepper a lot. He even thought that a friendship might be blossoming between them. She was spirited and friendly, not to mention very attractive, but there was no "It" factor between them. It was strictly platonic. Funny how that worked. There really was no rhyme or reason to sexual attraction, you either were or you weren't.

By the book, it would look like they would be the perfect match, same age, both single, both horse people, attractive, vibrant, but nope, totally in the friend zone. Now Annie, on the other hand, was like a bomb going off in his psyche. There was no doubt about it, she had completely bypassed the friend zone the second he had laid eyes on her.

Unfortunately, he would have to cool his heels until after she had fulfilled her bridesmaid duties at her friend's wedding on Saturday. For now, he had to focus on his mile-long list of responsibilities; there was no time to daydream. After calling Cal to inform him that he had the job, he got up from his desk and left to find Slim. They had fence to repair and miles to go before he could call it a day.

CHAPTER 11

*A*nnie helped Abbey into her wedding gown, recruiting Madeline to help. Annie laughed as Madeline appeared to get swallowed up in the layers of fabric. "Now we can add the train," Annie said.

Stepping back, they both eyed their handiwork. "You look amazing." Annie said to Abigail.

"I'm a nervous wreck." she replied.

"You've got this," Annie said.

"Are you sure?"

Looking at Abbey's terrified expression, Annie said, "Normal jitters, everyone goes through it."

The wedding party were all ready and waiting to walk down the aisle. The adorable flower girl and equally cute ring bearer, Annie the maid of honor, the bridesmaids and groomsmen, were fully decked out in their wedding attire and waiting for the moment they had rehearsed for.

"Come here everyone, let's form a circle," Annie commanded as they all gathered around the bride,

"Everyone hold hands. Abbey, we are all here, standing with you, supporting you, and surrounding you with our love. You are getting ready to embark on an incredible journey with the man you love, who adores you and is waiting for you." She paused, feeling choked up, "This is a moment in time that I hope you will never forget. My wish is for you to be fully present, savor the love all around you, take it in. You will never experience this time and moment again. I love you my friend, now go out and seal the deal." Just as Annie had hoped, they all laughed at the last comment just as the wedding march began to play.

～

*a*nnie arrived at the farm right on time for their one o'clock date in her cherry-red convertible. A young, good-looking, blond guy commented enthusiastically as she stepped out, "Nice car!"

"Thanks, it's a blast to drive," she said. Her cheeks were flushed, and hair wildly tossed from her ride with the top down.

"A car for a peacock if ya were to ask me," Slim grumbled to himself but not quite low enough to escape Annie's ears.

"Excuse me?" she said defensively, "I've worked my butt off for that car."

"Kinda car that's fer showoffs," he declared.

"Did someone get out from the wrong side of the bed this morning or are you always this rude?" Annie said huffily.

"Ain't rude iffin' it's the truth," he asserted.

"That's your opinion." she said, feeling more irritated by the second.

At that moment, Gabe walked out from the interior of the barn. Catching sight of Annie, he stopped dead in his tracks, comically clutching at his heart as he took several steps back.

"Annie you're here. I didn't hear you drive up. Is it possible that you've become even more stunning?" he said, as he approached her.

"Thank God someone is glad to see me," she said, while mentally approving of his black cowboy hat and the way he filled out his blue jeans in all the right places. His skin was already a golden tan, and the warmth of his gaze made her feel a little weak-kneed. His lighthearted countenance and innate confidence were very sexy indeed.

"I see you've already met Slim and Cal," he said.

"Not formally," Cal said stepping forward to offer his hand for a welcoming shake. "I'm Cal, it's a pleasure to meet you," he said staring at her admiringly.

"Nice to meet you too, Cal," she said, smiling warmly.

"This is Slim, my right-hand man," Gabe said formally introducing the crotchety old ranch hand.

"We met. Slim takes exception to my mode of transportation," she said, tattling.

"Oh, don't mind Slim, he's got lots of opinions, don't ya Slim?" Gabe said. "I hope you weren't giving Annie a hard time."

"Nope, not unless she has skin as thin as terlit paper," he said, grinning at his own joke.

"Oh, so that was a joke?" Annie said.

"No, I reckon I meant it," Slim replied.

"At least you're honest," Annie said.

"I see where this is heading… why don't we mosey on over to the pasture and bring our horses in," Gabe said, taking Annie's hand in his.

Annie turned to Cal and gave him a wide smile saying, "Thanks for the warm welcome."

He winked at her and nodded, leaning in to whisper conspiratorially, "I know the feeling."

Annie laughed as she and Gabe walked away to grab their halters and bring their rides in to saddle up.

"You remember Whiskey and Gil, don't you?" he asked as they returned from the field with their mounts.

"Of course," she replied, then began cooing to Whiskey, "Who could forget such a handsome fella?" Scratching him behind his ear she continued, "I rode Gil the last time and we really bonded."

While Annie was picking Whiskey's hooves, Cal came out carrying Whiskey's saddle.

"Why thank you Cal, that is so sweet of you," she said.

"No problem, I'm always happy to help out if I can," he said winking at her again.

"Let me cinch it up for ya," he said after placing the saddle and pad on the horse's back.

"You are a real sweetheart," Annie exclaimed.

"Hey now, I was going to get your saddle, Cal beat me to it," Gabe said not to be outdone by Cal.

"I'm sure you were," Annie teased.

"Cal don't you have work to do?" Gabe said.

"Sure boss, I'm on my way," he replied. "Bye Annie, it was a pleasure to meet you."

"Likewise," she said.

"He seems really nice," Annie commented after Cal

had disappeared into the barn.

"Yeah, he's new. I hired him this week. He seems to be working out fine."

"Maybe a little of his charm will rub off on Slim," she said.

"Doubtful," Gabe said and laughed.

"Just a thought."

Gabe gave her a leg up onto Whiskey before jumping onto his palomino. "Whiskey has been on stall arrest for a hoof abscess, but he seems solid now. He'll be glad to get out on the trails."

Gabe jumped onto his horse's back and said, "Are you ready to show this beautiful lady the countryside, Gil?" Gil nickered his response and they took their leave, trotting down the trail leading into the woods.

"It's as peaceful and beautiful as I remembered," Annie said as they wove their way through the trees along the well-trodden path.

Annie loved following Gabe; she had the best seat in the house, watching his broad shoulders and sexy butt move as one with his horse. His old black cowboy hat perched on top of his head, his faded blue jeans accentuating his lean body to perfection, she was having a moment for sure. The clip clop of the horses' hooves was hypnotic yet at the same time invigorating. She felt content yet excited. Gabe turned around in his saddle to look back at Annie, his grin revealing his joy.

"How long have you been riding?" Gabe asked.

"Since before I can even remember," Annie said, "It was my greatest escape from an unhappy home life, the thing that fed my soul and kept me sane when I was a kid," she shared.

"Yeah, same here, my older brother and me spent

every summer from dawn until dusk either riding or mucking stalls, repairing fence, whatever was needed. It probably saved our lives."

"Where did you grow up?" she asked wanting to know every single detail about his life.

"About an hour north of here, but our summers were spent at my grandparent's farm in Kentucky. My Mom couldn't wait to get rid of us. The minute school let out we were shipped off. I can't say that I blame her, we were a pair of wild asses," he admitted, laughing at himself.

"What about your dad?" she asked.

"Never knew him. He ran out on us after I was born, I guess the domestic life didn't suit him," he said. "My mom raised us all by her lonesome working as a waitress, no help from him, once he ditched us, we never heard from him again."

"I'm sorry Gabe, that must have been hard."

"They say you can't miss what you never had but I beg to differ, I missed my dad every single day of my childhood and beyond. His absence had as much influence as his presence would have, only not in the way I wanted. I vowed if I ever had children, I would give it 100 percent, no shortcuts," he declared. "My mom and my grandparents did their best to fill in the gaps though. They loved us fiercely, still do...my mom, she died five years ago from breast cancer, soon after her fiftieth birthday," he said. "We were all devastated, I still miss her."

"That must have been tough, raising two boys all on her own, and you not having a father around."

"Honestly, I've learned as much about how I want to live my life from what I don't want as what I do."

"Preach." Annie said.

"Oh, I'm good at pontificating just ask all my exes," he joked.

"And…how many exes are there?" she asked, curious to see how he would answer.

"Now I reckon that's a trick question," he said, as he laughed out loud. "I may be an ole cowpoke, but I know quicksand when I see it."

"Okay secret squirrel, have it your way," she said, playfully pouting. "Back to your family, is your brother still around?

"He actually moved to Kentucky after high school to be close to our grandparents and chose a career in accounting. Ha. Go figure, hard to fathom if you'd known him from his hell raisin' days. I'd go crazy being cooped up indoors looking at a computer or calculator all day. What about you? Are your parents still around?" he asked.

"Nope, both my parents are gone. Drank themselves to death," she said matter-of-factly. "Truth be told, my sister Darcy practically raised me. My parents didn't want another kid, I was a drunken night's mistake, and my mom certainly never failed to remind me of that. I was the youngest of four girls and my sisters spoiled me rotten, so I think that compensated for my parent's lack…like you said, sometimes we're shaped more by what could have been rather than what was."

"How could anyone not want you? That is unfathomable to me," Gabe said.

"I know, right? What's not to love?" she said, attempting to lighten the mood.

"I, for one, haven't discovered anything," he replied. "Not to change the subject but I packed a killer picnic lunch for us, and we'll be at the river before you know it."

"I can't wait, I skipped breakfast this morning. Gabe, thank you so much for this," she said.

"An opportunity to get out on Gil with a beautiful woman is no hardship, I'm happier than a Kentuckian on Derby day," he said.

As they wound their way down to the river, they startled some pheasants, which in turn surprised their mounts, who after a few quick side steps, took their cue from their riders, and returned to their previous confidence.

"Here we are, let's dismount and spread our blanket out," Gabe said. He looked around, always in awe of this sacred land no matter how many times he visited here. The mammoth and majestic sycamore trees reached far into the sky. The river, swollen from the spring rain, lent its soothing sound of rushing water to their magical day. The birds were mostly quiet this time of day, but the occasional sound of gold finches and white-throated sparrows serenaded them.

Gabe hopped off Gil then helped Annie dismount. They replaced the bridles with halters and let them graze. Gabe spread the thick army blanket on a flat spot he had searched out and unpacked his saddle bag.

"What a feast," Annie exclaimed as her mouth watered in anticipation.

Gabe had purchased submarine sandwiches from the local deli, along with homemade potato salad, grapes, chips and pickles.

"A picnic isn't complete without a piece of fresh baked apple pie," Gabe said, proudly displaying two huge pieces with crumbles on top.

Annie sat on the blanket and removed her socks and boots. Gabe watched her wiggle her bare toes, now released from their confinement. The sun warmed them as the spring breeze simultaneously kept them cool.

Gabe, balancing on one leg at a time, followed Annie's lead and removed his boots and socks. He then plopped down beside her, and wasted no time pulling her into his arms. He gently pushed her onto her back and swung his leg over hers, effectively pinning her to the blanket, and hovered over her as he gently kissed her.

"Oh Annie, I have waited all week for this moment," he said softly. He brushed her hair back from her brow and studied her. Looking into her hooded green eyes, he wavered between keeping a tight rein on his desire for her or total abandon. His pent-up longing won the battle, restraint and logic losing by a landslide.

He dipped his head and coaxed her lips apart, while cupping one hand behind her neck and running his other up and down her bare arm, enjoying the feel of her soft skin. The kiss was gentle, exploratory, meant to seduce, and it worked. He could feel her body melt against his own.

She wrapped her arms around his neck, deepening the kiss as she slipped her tongue into his mouth. He groaned as his penis hardened. Pulling back, he knew if he didn't put the brakes on now, it would take superpowers he wasn't sure he possessed to stop it from becoming something they might later regret.

Gabe rolled onto his side, propped up on his crooked elbow, the other arm draped across her waist; his large hand splayed her rib cage, almost touching her breast. Seeing his desire mirrored in her eyes, he had to touch her.

Slipping his hand under her tee shirt, he rolled his thumb over her nipple nestled inside the silky bra. She arched her back, pressing her breast further into his hand, inviting him to fondle her. Her cheeks were flushed, and she licked her lips as she moaned, prompting Gabe to cover her mouth again with his own. She tasted like maraschino cherries.

With extreme difficulty, Gabe managed to pull himself away from the ledge, "Oh, Annie girl, you could make a man go crazy," he rolled onto his back, his biceps flexing as he ran his hands through his hair.

Annie sat up, looking flushed and sexy as hell. With a slightly unsteady hand she reached for a grape and plucked it from its stem. She pressed it against Gabe's lips staring intently into his eyes. He licked and suckled her fingers as he took the fruit into his mouth. His eyes burned as he watched her grab another one for herself. Intentionally seducing him, she parted her full lips to sink her teeth into the ripe purple berry. Smiling seductively, she knew full well the effect she was having on him and was enjoying it immensely.

"Annie, I'm warning you now, you are playing with fire here," he said, voice ragged with desire.

"I like to live dangerously."

"Game on," he said, "But first we eat."

"If you say so." She pulled out one of the subs from its wrapper and took a huge bite. "Hmm, so good," she said talking with her mouth full.

It was such a quick turnaround that Gabe guffawed. She enchanted him, and it took everything in him not to grab the sub from her hands and kiss her again. But he knew he had to back off, or risk coming on way too hard, way too fast, way too soon. It was proving to be quite a challenge.

After finishing their lunch, they were too full to move and laid on the blanket talking. She loved the feel of being held in his arms with her cheek resting against his chest. She nuzzled his body enjoying his masculine scent, soap, Old Spice, and a hint of horse. Lying there, feeling his heartbeat, the steady rhythm of his breath, along with the cadence of his voice as he told her stories, lulled her into a light sleep. She didn't know how long she dozed before he gently kissed her awake.

"Wake up sleepy-head," Gabe said.

"I'm sorry, how long was I out?"

"Long enough to scare off the wild critters with all the snoring," he said grinning.

"I did not snore!" she said punching him lightly. "Did I?"

"I'm just teasing ya. It was about a half-hour cat nap. I mighta' dozed a little myself. We'd best get going."

"I wish we could stay here forever."

Gabe looked around, "It's beautiful, isn't it?"

"Yes, and we didn't have to travel thousands of miles to find it. It's right in your back yard," she said. They reluctantly packed up and headed back to the barn.

Both were quiet on the ride home, Annie feeling quite melancholy and wishing the day didn't have to end and Gabe wondering when he would have another opportunity to spend time with Annie.

Between his workload managing the farm and the new horse he was taking on; time would be at a premium. He didn't care—if she was willing to see him again, he would find the time… somehow.

CHAPTER 12

The Diamond was closed on Mondays, and it gave Annie much needed time to catch up on her laundry and spend some quality time with her neglected furry charges. She was still floating on a cloud from her date with Gabe the previous day.

She wasn't sure where this was heading, she only knew that she had never felt this way about any man before. Her senses were so heightened that the grass appeared greener, the sky a more vivid blue, the stars brighter, the food tastier... *Get a grip!* She knew she had better snap out of it soon, because she wasn't sure how serious Gabe was. Best to proceed with caution.

He was in a band for God's sake. He had women throwing themselves at him all the time. For all she knew he might just want a roll in the hay. Whatever was the case, she decided not to overthink and enjoy it.

Gabe was playing with his band on Friday night at a local bar, and he'd invited her to meet him there. He would put her on the guest list, plus one, in case she wanted to bring a friend along. She was excited to hear him play again and he had promised to take a real long set break to hang out with her. She didn't know if she could wait until then to see him, but she had to try. *Bye girl.* She had it bad.

Annie slipped on a pair of tennis shoes, grabbed three leashes from the hall closet and whistled for the dogs to follow her out to Darcy's van. A nice hike in the woods was what the doctor ordered. Nothing could straighten her out faster than being out in nature.

She loaded up the ecstatic canines and headed to the nearby state park.

~

*H*eading over to her place felt weird. She had only been back twice since Darcy had left two weeks ago. Soon she would be back in her own house getting used to living alone again. She loved having the dogs for company and knew someday when her schedule wasn't so hectic, she would have a couple of her own. Her ultimate dream was to have a horse as well…she knew that would be a long way off. She had to admit that being around horses again was a bonus to dating Gabe.

She grappled with her keys and finally unlocked the door to her condo. Her house smelled stale and it had an eerily vacant feel to it. Normally the southwest decor and color palette of her place soothed her senses and created a safe and cozy haven. Now it seemed like a hollowed-out shell, not a home at all. The opposite of how she usually felt when she returned home.

She put her purse on the entryway bench and

headed to her kitchen to grab the watering can for her thirsty plants. *Mental note to self, water the plants twice a week. They look pathetic.*

She glanced through her mail while the container filled with water. Nothing to get excited about except for a couple of greeting card-sized envelopes with no return address. She put the letters and bills aside to tend to her flora. "You poor little things," she said to her wilting houseplants, "I am terrible and I don't deserve you."

After watering she went upstairs to pick up extra underclothes and a couple pairs of shorts. She had a weird sense that someone had been in her bedroom. Nothing she could put her finger on, but a creepy feeling, and she felt the hair on the back of her neck tingle. She noticed that a photograph on her dresser of herself with Darcy looked out of place from how she remembered it.

Quit being paranoid. She still couldn't shake the feeling, so she hastily grabbed a small suitcase, threw in the items she needed, and quickly headed back downstairs. Damn she wished she had thought to bring one of the dogs with her. Her cell phone rang. It was Gabe.

"Hello."

"Hi Babe, how's your day going?""

"Trying to catch up with my life. Right now, I'm at my place grabbing a few things to take back to Darcy's," she said. "How about you? Any news about the horse?"

"Yes, they called a little while ago—I got the job. They'll trailer her here this Wednesday," he said, barely containing his excitement.

"That's fantastic Gabe. I am so happy for you. I can't wait to meet this million-dollar hay muncher."

"Only worth a million if I can help her. I'm going to have my work cut out for me with this one," he said. "From my understanding, she is in pretty bad shape. A truck hauling her mama and her, along with a few other horses, was in a terrible accident along the highway and the trailer overturned. Her mama, a champion worth a ton of money, and one of the other champion horses, were injured so badly they had to be put down at the scene. Midnight came out with only a few scratches but a lot of emotional scars. I only hope I'm up for the job."

"Gabe if anyone can help, it's you," Annie said.

"I hope so, I hate to see any horse suffering," he admitted.

"I have full confidence in you."

"I'll be relying on that," he said quietly. Her heart skipped a beat at the implications of that statement. He continued, "I'm looking forward to seeing you Friday, but I'm missing you now, and Friday seems like a million years away. Any chance that you could go see a movie with me tonight?" he asked.

"I'd love that," she said, without hesitation.

"Great, I'll pick you up around seven, if that's alright. The movie starts at seven thirty."

"I'll be ready, see you then."

"Hot damn, I get to see my girl tonight," he said.

Annie's heart flew into the stratosphere upon hearing him say, "My girl." She hastily said goodbye and hung up the phone. Only after disconnecting did she realize she didn't even know what movie they were going to see, but frankly she didn't give a damn. For all she cared, they could be going to see *Friday the 13th* and she hated horror films. She couldn't wait to see him again.

Returning to the kitchen, she checked the back door only to find that it was unlocked. *What next?* Annie was sure she'd secured it when she left the last time. She usually triple-checked herself when it came to that. She must be losing it. *Okay, I'm getting the hell out of here, now I'm really creeped out.* She hurriedly locked the back door, grabbed her things and headed to the front entrance.

As she reached the door, she saw the doorknob turning clockwise, then counterclockwise, then back again. Someone was trying to get in. Now she was in full freak-out mode. She had secured the deadbolt but must not have turned the lock on the doorknob itself. Panicked, she backed away from the door stumbling, as she tried to override her shaking hands to dial 911.

As she finally steadied her tremors enough to push the buttons on her phone, there was an accompanying knock at the door, followed by a familiar voice, "Hey anybody in there?" It was Bradley.

Relief flooded her nervous system as she quickly unlatched the deadbolt and opened the door. "Bradley, thank God it's you! You scared the crap out of me. What are you doing here anyway?" she said in a rush.

"On duty and cruising the neighborhood. Where have you been? You haven't been home for a couple of weeks," he said. "Are you seeing someone?" he asked.

"Bradley, even if I am it's none of your business," she replied.

"Well, are you?"

"I have been out with a guy a couple of times, nothing serious," she added.

"It must be serious if you aren't sleeping in your own bed," he said.

"No, Bradley if you must know I am dog sitting for Darcy while she and Sam are on vacation," she replied impatiently. "Again, it should be of no concern to you anyway."

"I wanted to make sure you are safe, living here all alone... It's my responsibility to protect you. Annie, I know you will eventually come around to seeing that what we had was special. I'll be patient. You're worth the wait."

"I've got to go. Please Bradley, move on, you must let go. This relationship is over. I don't know how else to convince you," she pleaded. "Maybe you should consider therapy as a way to get the support you need, to help you to get on with your life."

"Are you trying to tell me I'm nuts?" he said, laughing. "Therapy is for weak people. I am the last person that needs therapy."

"Listen, I have to go now, the dogs have been cooped up too long, I'll see you around."

"When?" he asked.

"I don't know," she answered. "I'll call you sometime," she said.

"Annie, Annie, Annie, I'm not going to accept that for an answer, you'll have to better than that," he said.

"I'll call you this week, please I have to go now," she said, becoming more uncomfortable every second.

"I'll be waiting. I have to get back on the clock anyway, duty calls." His black-as-night eyes burned with intensity.

It was becoming apparent that Bradley lived in a fantasy world all his own making, and she needed to be extra vigilant. She decided at that moment to stop at the pharmacy on her way home to pick up some pepper spray.

∼

*G*abe arrived promptly at seven and Annie was ready and waiting. He had called to let her know that he was picking her up on his motorcycle, and to dress accordingly. Her green eyes sparkled with anticipation as she opened the door for Gabe who was standing at the threshold. She threw the dogs a treat and closed the door, locking it behind her.

"I hope my jean jacket is enough of a wind barrier," she said, doubtfully.

"You'll be fine, if you get cold you can wear my jacket."

She hiked her leg over the bike as he steadied it for her. Gabe climbed on in front of her and opted to kick start the Harley Sportster rather than use the magic button. It rumbled to life and he carefully backed it around to face the road before they took off.

She wrapped her arms loosely around his leather-clad waist and relaxed her body so that she could move with the bike. She felt so carefree in that moment and so feminine, kind of like Jane with Tarzan, and was surprised to find that she liked the feeling. He was so confident in everything he did and his skill handling the bike was no exception. It was such a turn on. Snuggling her pelvis against his back she relaxed and enjoyed the ride.

∼

*G*abe reached for Annie's hand and interlaced his fingers with hers as they crossed the street to get in the line for their movie tickets. There were about half dozen people ahead of them for a new-release romantic comedy starring Jennifer Aniston, one of Annie's favorite actors. They made small talk with the couple in front of them, but all Annie could concentrate on was the electricity from Gabe's hand holding hers and how incredibly sexy he was.

She had to force herself to quit staring at him. His wide white smile dazzled her. Honestly, he could charm a snake from its burrow. When his eyes met hers, they held a warmth that made her toes curl. She hadn't even been aware she had such a longing inside herself, but now it pervaded her entire being.

Upon entering the cinema, Gabe tugged her along to the concession stand and perused the candy display like a twelve-year-old kid. He smiled at the awkward teenager taking his order, who proceeded to blush a deep crimson and looked as if she wanted to crawl under the counter and hide.

"We'd like a big tub of buttered popcorn, a bag of Twizzlers, and a box of Milk-duds please. Oh, and an extra-large Pepsi," he looked at Annie with a big grin, "Now what would you like? I'm willing to share… what is your favorite?"

"I think you've got it covered," she said approving of his choices. "Milk-duds and Twizzlers are my favorite."

"I guess that's it then," he said, smiling at the young girl.

"Extra butter?" the clerk managed to croak out.

"Yeah, why not," he grinned at her, "and thank ya."

"Sure." She blushed fire engine red from Gabe's attention before adding the extra butter and setting it on the counter next to the rest of the booty.

"That will be fifty dollars," Annie whispered in Gabe's ear giggling.

"Wouldn't be surprised," he agreed. "It's worth it though; it always tastes better at a movie theater."

"It's true." Annie said smiling.

The previews for the coming attractions were already playing when they entered the dark auditorium. "Front, middle, or back?" Gabe whispered in her ear.

"Back," she answered immediately.

They took middle seats in the very back row and hunkered down together. Popcorn in Gabe's lap, drink in the holder, candy in Annie's bag, comfortable seats, sirens going off in Annie's nervous system, best date night ever.

Between movie trailers, all you could hear were wrappers crumpling and people munching on their popcorn. Annie had to stifle a giggle. Gabe put his arm across her shoulders hugging her to him and said, "I feel like I'm on my very first date, and about sixteen years old again."

"Me too," Annie replied softly. "It feels kinda good."

"Strangely enough it does, although I wouldn't go back to my teens again for anything." He kissed the top of her head as the featured film began.

"Thanks for picking out a chick flick," she said.

"Don't tell anyone, my reputation will be shattered," he said.

"Your secret is safe with me." They settled into the intimacy of the moment, as if only she and Gabe existed and everything else had slipped away. She leaned her head into the crook of his arm, her head resting against his chest, and breathed in the manly scent of him, earthy with a hint of aftershave and laundry soap. She wondered if she would be able to remember anything about this film, but she had no doubt she would remember everything about their date.

CHAPTER 13

Bradley pounded his fist on the steering wheel in a rage as he drove around town. After hearing that Annie was staying at her sister's, he had staked it out after he got off duty and had seen lover-boy ride up on his motorcycle and whisk her away. He had followed them in his gray truck, keeping a safe distance and remaining undetected.

He fucking knew it. How could she? He saw her looking all googly eyed at him in the ticket line. Smiling up at him, holding hands. He struck his dashboard again. She used to look at him like that. She would again, he was sure of it.

He intended to find out who the hell this guy was, trying to steal his girl. He could forgive her, but him, well that was another story.

Bradley decided to stop in and have a beer at Finnegan's, a local bar, and wait out the movie. Maybe shoot a round or two of pool to cool his temper off. Slamming his truck door shut, he strode angrily into the bar and ordered a tall one from the bartender, who called him by name since he was a regular.

The cop crowd often hung out here when off-duty, and Bradley could always count on seeing a familiar face. He noticed a woman he had recently shared a wild night of sex with, he thought her name was Dee, smiling seductively at him. It wasn't Annie, but he could close his eyes and pretend it was for a night of sex. A man had his needs. Hopefully Dee would still be around after he got back from seeing that Annie arrived home safely.

The woman in question got up from her bar stool and came over to Bradley, making sure he had the perfect vantage point for viewing her ample cleavage, almost spilling out from her tight knit top. "Hey Sexy, where have you been? You said you would call," she pouted sexily.

"I've been busy, but I'm here now. I've got an errand to run in a little while, but if you wait here for me, we can go back to my place and pick up where we left off," he said tantalizing her with his intense dark eyes.

"I'll be here," she replied breathlessly.

"Want to shoot a game of pool?" he asked.

"Sure, let me go get my purse," she said swinging her hips as she returned to the bar, with more than a few men lustfully watching her walk.

Score, Bradley thought to himself, *that was too damn easy.* He strode to the pool table to put his quarters up.

abe left Annie reluctantly, with her promise that she would be at his show on Friday night. He had dialed it down after a few kisses, knowing he wanted much more than a fling.

Annie was something special, not like any other woman he had ever been with. She was making him rethink his partying ways. Despite what his bandmates thought, Gabe felt lonely at times and one-night stands were as lonely as it got as far as Gabe was concerned. He had learned that a long time ago.

He was so engrossed with his thoughts that it took a moment to realize that a truck had come up behind him. Way too close. It had seemingly come out of nowhere and was now hugging his ass. Gabe went full throttle and pulled away only to have the truck gun its motor and come right back up on him again. Now he was pissed, and his adrenaline surged. Speeding up even more, he tried to outrun the truck, but it kept right on his tail. By this point he only hoped a cop would miraculously show up, because he was beginning to panic.

What the fuck! This guy must be insane, he's trying to run me off the fucking road. Up ahead was his turn off to the farm but he was moving too fast to take it, so he passed on by. As suddenly as it had appeared, the truck backed off, braked, and sped off the way they'd come, the only evidence the red taillights disappearing into the darkness. *Now what the hell was that about?* Hands shaking from the rush, he pulled over for a moment to steady himself, then turned back and headed home.

Later, tossing and turning in bed, he envied Sam's dogs, Bella and Mimi, who were already snuggled up and fast asleep… he was still way too wired to doze off, and knew he would probably hear the roosters crow before he even got a wink of sleep.

CHAPTER 14

*T*oday was the big day, and Gabe estimated that Midnight would arrive within the hour, as he checked his watch for the umpteenth time. Gabe had an inner buzz of excitement for this latest challenge. This was what he was born to do, it gave him a sense of purpose. Other than his music, helping horses to overcome their issues and gain self-confidence was the most satisfying life experience he knew of. It could often be the difference between life and death for these magnificent beings.

"Hope you know what yer gittin in fer," Slim said.

"Yeah, me too," Gabe said.

"If I was to be bettin on you or the horse, I'd put my money on you, and that's the dern truth," Slim said.

"I'll be damn; I think you paid me a compliment Slim," Gabe said.

"Now don't git yer boots all dusty dancing the jig," Slim replied, offering a rare smile.

"Wouldn't think of it," Gabe said, adding, "You know

Slim, I'm going to be counting on you more than ever with me taking on this latest project, I hope you don't mind."

"I got ya covered," Slim said, "I'm gonna go check on them water troughs and open the back gate, okay with you?" Slim asked.

"Sure, stick close by, I may need your help getting Midnight settled in. I thought I would turn her out in the north pasture by herself and put Whiskey in the paddock next to her. I may work in the round pen with her this afternoon. Whiskey has a way with the ladies, and I'm hoping he'll be a good welcoming committee," he said, grinning.

"Not a bad idear," Slim said with grudging approval as he walked off to complete his chores.

Gabe walked out to the field where he would be turning Midnight loose and studied the area. Plenty of pasture for Midnight to let off a little steam. He would let her run and kick up her heels for a while before getting acquainted in the round pen. Whiskey was as steady as they come and seemed to be a calming influence on the whole herd. He knew she was going to need a friend.

On his way back to the tack room to get a halter and lead rope to wrangle Whiskey in, he looked down. Frowning, he stooped down to pick up a discarded cigarette butt from the barn aisle. Gabe shook his head in disgust as he slipped the butt into his shirt pocket. He knew he would have to get to the bottom of it, but he'd have to wait until later. Right now, he had a traumatized little filly arriving and he needed to prepare her new digs.

~

"She's here!" Gabe called out. Cal and Slim joined Gabe in watching the luxury horse trailer make its way down the long gravel lane. As the truck got closer, they could hear kicking and stomping coming from the rear of the trailer and loud snorts followed by a screaming roar of rage. The driver parked and killed the engine. Gabe went into instant action. Walking to the back of the trailer he began talking softly to the terrified and angry horse. The driver hopped out of the truck and met Gabe at the rear of the carriage.

"Hi, I'm Gabe Hunter, must have been a long ride with all that carrying on," he said sticking out his hand for a friendly shake.

"I'm Russ," he said. "I don't envy you none. I've had to listen to this almost the entire trip here," Russ complained. "If they'd asked me, which they didn't, I would have recommended the glue factory. This filly is a lost cause as far as I'm concerned," he said.

"Every horse deserves a chance," Gabe replied.

"Be careful, and don't go getting yourself killed trying," Russ cautioned.

"That's the plan," Gabe said. "You mind if I unload her?" Gabe asked.

"Have at it," Russ replied. "I'll let you go in through the side door and when you're ready I'll open the back-trailer gate."

"Slim, go secure the front gate in case she gets away from me, Cal I'll need you to stand by the rear as she backs out, not too close," Gabe instructed. Gabe disappeared into the trailer and could be heard having a conversation with his new trainee.

"Now aren't you a beautiful filly. Midnight, you and me, we need to come to a little understanding here. I'm on your side, we're going to be getting real close you and I, and I'm the best friend you'll ever have," he said in a calming voice. Snorts could be heard as the horse pawed at the trailer bed.

"Oh, so you're not having it, I get it girl, but I'm here to tell ya that it's going to be alright," he continued in his soothing tone, then called out to Russ, "Okay go ahead and open 'er up."

He held on to the lead rope with gloved hands, as Midnight backed out of the trailer with Gabe following, the rope taunt. The instant she was on solid ground she reared up, pawing the air.

"Whoa, steady, steady girl," Gabe said as she continued to rear and squeal. "Get back Cal, everybody, step back," he said moving his body slowly while swinging the rope in circles to get her attention. He knew getting the horse to move her feet would make her pay more attention to him than her fear. Her ears started to move, and she slowly began to focus on Gabe. After gaining her attention and distracting her enough, he was able to lead her to the pasture.

"Good girl," he murmured. He stroked her neck as he removed the lead rope from her halter. He laughed as she immediately took off at a gallop kicking up her back heels and bucking as she went.

"Wow. She is a beauty." Cal said, joining Gabe, Slim and Russ, who were watching the spectacle. Whiskey called out to Midnight, her ears perked up and she headed straight over to the fence to investigate her new friend.

"That she is," Gabe responded, already half in love with his newest trainee.

Gabe observed Midnight until she put her head down and began to graze, before turning back to walk Russ to his truck.

"Nice meeting you, Russ," Gabe said.

"Yeah, good luck and I mean that sincerely," he replied.

"Thanks, I think she and I are going to get along just fine," Gabe said.

"Now that I've seen you in action, I don't doubt it," he replied, jumping into his truck. Slim had reopened the gate and Russ wasted no time taking his leave.

"Slim, can I talk to you for a minute?" Gabe said.

"Whatcha waitin fer?" he grumbled.

Gabe reached into his shirt pocket and pulled out the discarded cigarette butt, holding it out so Slim could see it.

"Isn't this your brand?"

"So what iffin it is?" Slim said.

"I found this inside the barn. As a matter of fact, right in the aisle next to the bales of hay."

"I reckin I shouldn't have to tell ya that I ain't never smoked inside this barn or any other barn," he said huffily.

"Look I'm not accusing you Slim, but I found it there pure and simple, it's your brand, you're the only one I know of that smokes around here, what am I supposed to think?"

"You kin think whatever ya damn well please but I

ain't the one that left it there," he said, as he angrily stalked away.

"What was that all about?" Cal asked.

"Cal, do you happen to smoke?" Gabe responded with a question of his own.

"Nope, never have," he said.

"OK, that's good then," Gabe said, turning and heading back to his office.

CHAPTER 15

"Annie, she is magnificent. I've never seen a more beautiful horse," Gabe said, his excitement contagious.

"I can't wait to meet her," Annie said. She smiled into the phone at Gabe's enthusiasm.

"I already feel a connection with her, I know it will be a long road, but I have no doubt I can help her," he said.

"I know you will," Annie said.

"Listen, when you get to the bar on Friday, tell the bouncer you're with me, I'll make sure you are on the list," he said.

"Can't wait."

"Me either, seems like a month since I saw you, and it was only two days ago," Gabe said.

"I know," she agreed. "I am so looking forward to it. Frankly it will be the only thing getting me through the next two days of my grueling schedule. I don't know what I was thinking when I overbooked myself like this. I'm not sure how I'm going to make it," Annie said.

"I'm happy to be the danglin' carrot for ya. I'll see you Friday…and Annie?"

"Yes?"

"You're always near, no matter what I'm doing I feel you, sometimes you are like music turned way down low and then the next minute cranked up high, but the radio is always on, I miss you."

"Night Gabe," she replied softly.

"Night Annie."

Annie paused after hanging up the phone, wondering where this budding romance was going to lead her. She hadn't been expecting it, nor had she asked for it, yet here it was…she could feel her heart opening to this man a little more each day. She had never been a slouch in the confidence department, but then, she had never had to compete for a man's attention. She felt a bit intimidated by the inevitable groupies that were sure to follow a guy as gorgeous and charming as Gabe.

She had a feeling she would be tested, as would Gabe. She guessed that was the name of the game when it came to romantic entanglements. Each had their challenges. Time would tell if they would be able to go the distance and it was much too soon to speculate for that matter. Sighing, she turned the television volume back up, refocusing on her favorite house fixer upper show.

All three dogs chose that moment to raise a ruckus, barking at something real or imagined lurking in the backyard. She got up from the couch to investigate, peering out into the dark night.

"What is it guys?" she said. "What's got your hair

standing up? Hmm? You are the very best watch dogs. Good babies," she said praising them. "So brave, you want a biscuit?"

Their ears immediately perked up at the word biscuit, only Fannie remained warily focused on the backyard.

"It's OK girl, come get your treat. There is nothing to worry about," she said as Fannie let out a deep and menacing low growl, one that made the hair on Annie's neck tingle.

"You're creeping me out." she told her canine companion. Annie strained to see in the dark night, but nothing looked out of order, so she crossed her fingers that there were no skunks and let the dogs outside, after calling out to scare off any unwanted critters. The dogs went tearing off at full speed toward the woods in the back corner of Darcy's lot.

Annie stepped outside in her night shirt to stand on the deck, the air cool against her bare legs. She loved being away from the city lights, the sky was so much darker and the stars so much brighter. She could see the Big Dipper, the Great Bear and the Little Bear.

One of the few good memories she had of her father was a camping trip he had taken she and her sisters on. Her mom, who hated camping, had stayed at home, so they had a rare chance to be alone with their dad. After setting up camp they had taken a night hike to an open field for sky watching. Spreading out the blanket they had brought along, they lined up on their backs, side by side, she, her three sisters, and their dad...Annie crossing her fingers and wishing with all her heart to see a shooting star.

That evening he had taught them how to find the

Great Bear by finding the Big Dipper's handle, which was the Bear's tail. He then showed them that you could find The Great Dog by finding Orion, The Hunter. She had always held on to that memory of her father, he was so whimsical and kind to her that night, away from the toxic relationship he and her mother had shared, he had shown a tenderness that she held inside even all these years later. It made her feel sad that she had been cheated out of more moments like that with her father.

"See that Freddie? That cluster of stars is called the Great Dog, just like you," she said, laughing when he looked at her like he understood what she was saying. Whistling, she called the other two canines inside and closed and locked the sliding doors.

"Fannie girl, I told you there was nothing to worry about," she said. Turning the TV off she led the parade of four to the bedroom and the dogs quickly jumped onto the king-sized mattress. They were already snoozing when Annie joined them a few minutes later. She fell asleep immediately without giving another thought to the dogs' earlier warning.

CHAPTER 16

"Knock knock," Pepper called out to Gabe as she entered his cluttered office. "Looks like you're in the thick of it.

"Pretty much," he laughed, "What can I do for ya?"

Pepper glanced furtively behind her then moved further into the office pulling the door shut, "I'm a little uncomfortable coming to you with this, and I absolutely hate tattling, but I thought you should be aware, a couple of times this week I have found the water trough overflowing with the hose still left on, then when I was throwing a flake of hay in for Kizzy, I found this tucked behind the bales," she said, pulling an empty pint bottle of Southern Comfort from under her shirt. "Maybe they aren't related but then again…"

"I see," Gabe said thoughtfully. "I'll take care of it, and your name will be left out of the conversation."

"I'm sorry, I know you already have a lot on your plate. Speaking of…when is Sam getting home?"

"Next Wednesday, thank God. Can't happen soon enough."

"I hope they had a great time. I can't imagine a whole month in Italy, can you? I turned Kizzy out, oh... and I shut off the water and rolled up the hose," Pepper said.

"Thanks Pepper, you did the right thing by coming to me," Gabe said.

"I hope so, everyone can make a mistake," she said. "I've got to go. I'm working the night shift again and I have to wash off the barn smells."

"Have a good night, see you soon, and thanks for the heads up," Gabe said.

"No problem, bye Gabe."

"Bye Pepper."

This was a part of the job that Gabe could do without. He didn't want to accuse anyone, but he knew he couldn't let it go. There was too much at stake; he had to deal with it. Of course, it was always possible that one of the kids he had hired for temporary help with the hay had tucked that empty bottle there, but knowing Slim's history with alcohol, he had to ask him about it. It would have to be handled delicately. Slim was proudly twenty years sober, but Gabe knew relapses were common even after many years of sobriety.

Even more troubling to Gabe was finding another cigarette butt by the back barn earlier this morning. It didn't make sense unless Slim was drinking again. He was the hardest and most conscientious worker he had ever known. He knew that back in Slim's drinking days, whiskey had been his vice of choice. Slim had lost everything and hit rock bottom before finally turning his life around by getting straight.

He would wait for the right moment this weekend to have the dreaded conversation, but in the meantime, the farrier was due to arrive within the next hour to shoe several of the horses that were boarded there. He'd have Cal bring them in and hold them while their shoes were put on, which would free up his time to work with Midnight.

Plunking his cowboy hat on, he went to find Cal. Midnight seemed to be adjusting and had already bonded with Whiskey, no surprise there, Gabe thought. At least some things were going right. Tonight, he would get to play with his band and see Annie. Now that sounded like a perfect combination. Spying Cal walking toward him, Gabe corralled him long enough to lay out the plan for this afternoon, then went to bring Midnight in for a training session.

When Gabe entered the pasture, he stood for a few minutes taking in the view. Rolling green hills dotted with mature trees, the bluest of skies, and big puffy clouds that seemed to float like hot air balloons. There she was, grazing, as black as coal and as shiny as obsidian, the most beautiful horse he had ever laid eyes on.

Gabe whistled then followed that by calling out Midnight's name and was encouraged to see her immediately raise her head from the grass and look his way. He called again and her ears pricked forward, then she nickered, and Gabe's heart melted.

"Come on girl, get on over here." She began to walk toward him as he held out his palm, bribing her with an oat treat which she happily accepted when she reached him. "You are a real sweetheart, aren't you? I won't let those big boogie men get you, you don't have to worry about a thing." His soft calming voice soothed her nervousness and he slipped on her halter. She nuzzled his neck and he felt his emotions rise. This filly had been through so much in her young life and yet, she still wanted to love and believe and trust. "Let's get to work girl, we have a long road ahead of us, but we've already come pretty damn far."

CHAPTER 17

"Hey Rocker, put that speaker over in the corner," Gabe instructed as he and the band set up their equipment. They were running a little behind and he wanted to make sure they had enough time for a decent sound check.

"Where do you want me to set up my drums?" he asked.

"I think the back-left corner, and Nate can set up in the opposite corner," Gabe said, referring to the keyboard player.

"Derek wants to do a couple of songs for the sound check since we're using the bar's sound equipment," Gabe said. He knew they were lucky to have Derek. He was an amazing sound technician and had the best ear he knew.

Jake and Billy jumped on stage, joking with each other about who was going to be the first to get the bartender to agree to go out with them.

"Don't you guys have something better to do?" Gabe asked.

"That's why we don't play drums, not much set up or tear down, what's your point amigo?" Billy said.

"My point is quit slacking and give us a hand, that will impress the bartender more than you two pounding your chests," he said.

"Billy listen to our wiseass…ahemm, I mean wise leader," Jake said, poking fun at Gabe.

"Ha ha ha. Listen, I've got an idea, why don't we dedicate one set just for you, so you can try out your comedy act. You are in the wrong lane dude—you need to be a standup comedian," Gabe said, giving it right back.

"Hey assholes could I have some help over here," Rocker called out as he lugged in another piece of heavy equipment. That was enough to motivate Billy and Jake, and in no time, they were set up and ready for their sound check.

"Testing one…two…three…" Gabe said into the microphone, "Hey Derek a little more sound to my mic, one…two…" then he began singing a couple bars of a line from a Jason Aldean song. He was right in the middle of a verse when the door opened, and Annie stepped through.

He stopped in midsentence. She was wearing a flirty short sundress in some aqua color, scooped low in the front, shoulders and arms bare, legs to die for, and cowboy boots. Her thick mane of red hair was loose and cascading down her back and shoulders. She was as stunning as any movie star he had ever seen.

"You guys finish your check I've got to go get my girl," he said as he leapt off the stage.

"Can I say, *wow?*" Gabe asked, pulling Annie into his arms.

"You look pretty delicious yourself," she said, smiling up at him.

"My my, you sure know how to throw a man off of his game."

"That's good because I'm not into games," Annie said.

He leaned in for a kiss—he had to. Her lips were soft and full, he lingered. Whispering against her mouth he said, "You taste like honey, and you smell like an orange blossom bush in full bloom, I have to have one more." He hungrily covered her mouth with his. The passion ignited between them instantly. She slipped her arms around his neck and opened her lips wider as his tongue plundered. His breath fast and ragged, he reluctantly pulled away, but kept his arms loosely around her waist his hands resting on her hips.

"I guess I had better get back up there with the band, we should be about ready for our first set," he said. "I hope you enjoy the show." He lightly brushed his lips across hers one last time, then returned to the stage. A crowd had gathered and as far as Annie was concerned, there were a few too many adoring females gawking at Gabe from the front row.

"Hey y'all thanks for coming out tonight. We have the best fans out there, it means a lot, really. If ya don't know, we're the Lonesome Cowpokes, I'm Gabe, we got Rocker on drums, Jake next to me on guitar, Nate playing keyboards, and Billy on bass. Can't go forgettin' our sound man back there, Derek, couldn't do it without him. Now let's get to what brought you all out in the first place..."

Gabe's smooth vocal tones reminded Annie of Jackson Browne, like melting butter, it was at once both soothing and sexy. She stood right in front of the stage holding a cold beer while swaying to the music. As the second song picked up, she was surprised to see Cal standing next to her.

"Cal. What are you doing here?" she laughed hugging him, glad for the company.

"Hey Annie, Gabe invited me, I hadn't heard them play before so here I am," he said.

"I am so happy to see you," she replied.

"Are you ready for another beer yet?" he asked.

"Sure, let me give you some money," Annie said.

"No, hell no." Cal turned to fight his way through the crowd to get them another round.

"I'd like to dedicate this next song to a very special lady, this one is for you, Annie," Gabe said, looking steadily at her as he began to sing Billy Currington's song, *Let Me Down Easy*. The song felt like it was now their song. The words touched her soul deeply, as they had when he sang to her in the truck. It was so seductive that she was completely, utterly, under his spell. Their gazes locked and he sang as if she were the only one in the room. Cal came up beside her, but she only had eyes for Gabe. The rest of the world had ceased to exist.

"Earth to Annie, here's your beer," Cal said, touching her arm to get her attention.

She smiled brightly at Cal and he almost stumbled back. "That Gabe is one lucky dude is all I can say," he said.

"Why thank you Cal," she said.

Gabe had moved on to the next tune, but his attention didn't stray far from Annie. She could almost feel the envious looks from the other women that were being slung her way and decided to soak it up and enjoy.

As the band began another song, Cal shyly asked Annie if she would dance with him. Looking at his earnest expression, she couldn't say no.

"Why not?" she replied.

He took her into his arms as if she were a delicate flower. "I won't break Cal, let's cut the rug."

"Cut the rug? What does that mean?"

Annie laughed, her eyes sparkling with mirth, "Never mind. It's an old-fashioned expression for kicking up our heels on the dance floor," she explained with another euphemism. "Oh, never mind, let's dance," she said pulling him closer and leading the dance. "Now dip me," she commanded.

He obliged and her head came close to the floor, then suddenly she was upright again with him twirling her around. They continued to act up and playfully try out new dance moves. "Oh, now I get it, you were holding out on me," she said, teasing Cal as the song finished.

Cal looked at her with such adoration that Annie realized how vulnerable and young he was. Maybe only a couple years younger than her chronologically, but light years younger emotionally. "Let's go to the bar and grab another beer," Annie said, hoping to change gears.

"Sounds good," Cal agreed.

On stage the band was almost done with the first set and Gabe said, "We're going to play one more song and then take a little break, but don't go anywhere we have a couple more sets for ya'll. Don't forget to grab one of our CDs or a tee-shirt. We have 'em on sale by the entrance, we'll be happy to sign your copy after the show. Don't forget to tip your servers."

They ended the set with an upbeat honkytonk song that left the crowd energized and wanting for more. Gabe made his way straight to Annie and Cal.

"You made it," Gabe greeted Cal.

"Yeah, you sound awesome."

"Thanks for taking care of my girl," Gabe said.

"It was tough, but someone had to do it."

"Everyone's a comedian tonight." He put his arm around Annie's waist and pulled her against his side. She slipped her arm around him, liking the feel of his body beneath her fingers, hard and all muscle. Leaning toward the bar, he ordered a beer for himself and another round for Cal and Annie. The female bartender was a little over-the-top flirtatious for Annie's liking, but Gabe didn't seem to notice.

He raised his bottle to the two of them for a toast, "Here's to new friends, romance, and beer," grinning as they clinked bottles.

Jake and Billy sidled up to get a couple of digs in on their friend, "Thanks for putting our love-sick bull moose out of his misery, earlier he was watching that dang door like his life depended on it," Billy said, then introduced himself and his sidekick. "This here is Jake and I'm Billy."

"Remember, I'm the funny one, right Gabe?" Jake said.

"No contest," Gabe retorted then leaned down to nibble Annie's ear lobe.

She giggled, high on his attention. It felt too damn good.

"This is Cal, my new hire at the farm, he's fitting in great. Lucky to have him," Gabe said making the introduction to his band mates.

"I'm the lucky one, I really appreciate you giving me the opportunity, I hope I can learn from you. You're a rising star in the horse world, I'm honored to be able to observe and learn from ya," he said.

"Don't believe everything you hear," Gabe said.

"Oh, he's a rising star alright, he is a regular Polaris," Jake said ribbing his friend with obvious affection.

"On that note we had better get back up there before everyone leaves," Gabe said. He kissed the tip of Annie's nose, "See you in a bit."

"I'll be here."

"Come backstage after this set so we can have a little privacy. It's right behind the stage the door on the right," he said, pointing.

"OK," she said.

"Annie? Hey what brings you here?" Annie turned toward the voice only to discover that it was Bradley's partner and best friend, Ike.

"Hi Ike, what are *you* doing here?" she asked.

"I'm out on a hot date. We met online. Here she comes now," he said as a young blond approached, no doubt coming from the restrooms.

"Sue this is Annie, Bradley's ex," he said by way of introduction.

"Hi, I've heard so much about you," Sue said holding out a slim hand toward Annie.

"Hi, I'm not sure if that is good or bad," Annie joked.

"Oh, Bradley still has it bad for you," she said,

creating an awkward moment as Ike gently nudged her with his elbow.

"On that note, I think we'll return to our table," Ike said. He glanced around the room like he was looking for someone, "Who are you here with?"

"I'm by myself but met up with some friends," she said, being deliberately vague.

"Hmm, if you say so," Ike said. "Who were all those guys you were talking to a few minutes ago?"

"What is this Ike, an interrogation?" Annie said. She felt slightly annoyed and not very happy to see him. She knew he'd immediately report back to Bradley that she had been there.

"No, I'm curious, it looked like you might be hanging out with the band and maybe a little tight with the singer," he said, grinning knowingly.

"Then why did you ask?" she said, now really annoyed.

"I'm happy for ya, Annie, he's every girl's dream don't ya think? And you're the lucky one that caught the big fish, at least for tonight anyway," he said. "Have fun." He winked and then followed Sue who had already headed back to their table.

Suddenly the joy had been sucked out of the evening. No good could come of this random meeting. Ike was another piece of work like his bestie Bradley— they were both arrogant assholes. She had never been fond of him.

This time she stayed at the bar for the whole set, rarely looking at Gabe during his performance. Ike was right, every girl's dream, and how long before the next beautiful woman caught his eye? What was she thinking? Cal returned from the dance floor where he had been making a connection with a pretty young woman. She thought Cal already had a girlfriend, but it was none of her business.

"Are you OK sitting here alone?" Cal asked.

"Of course, go have fun, this set will probably be over soon then I'll be meeting Gabe backstage," she said.

"If you're sure?"

"Yes, I'm sure."

The set ended shortly after and Annie made her way to the back room. The door was partially open, so she entered without knocking. She saw a young woman embracing Gabe. When he looked up and saw Annie, he pushed the blond beauty away, but it was too late.

"Oh, I'm sorry I interrupted." Annie said, as she quickly turned and ran from the room.

"Annie! Annie, come back!" Gabe said, as he rushed to catch up with her.

She had a head start and she ran out the door into the night, but Gabe was right on her heels.

"Stop, Annie, please, give me a chance to explain."

She turned, her cheeks pink with humiliation, "There is nothing to explain. You're a musician, you're a player, I've been played."

"No, no, *no*! Annie, I am sure it looked bad from your end but believe me there is nothing going on between me and that girl."

"Oh really? It looked pretty intimate to me," she said. "Who is she?"

"Her name is Robbie. We met at a gig; I had a meaningless one-night stand with her a long time ago."

"Is that how she sees it? A meaningless one-night stand?"

"Unfortunately, no. She fancies herself in love with

me, all fine and good except that she doesn't even know me. Look I screwed up, I thought we were both on the same page. We talked about it, but after the fact she said she had developed feelings for me. There is nothing going on between us, never was. I feel bad, but that's the truth."

"That's what scares me the most. You are surrounded by women who are crushing on you. What happens in a weak moment? Late night, lonely, a few beers, I'm not judging you, It's just that I'm aware of the temptations."

"She was the last one for me," Gabe said. "I knew that it was a mistake almost immediately, but I couldn't take it back."

"Annie, look at me," he said, and seeing the tears shimmering in her eyes said, "Baby," as he rubbed his thumb under her cheek where a tear had escaped. "Please listen, yes, I'm in a band, yes, I've had my share of meaningless flings, yes it takes a lot of confidence to be with a singer in a band, I know all of that, but I want more than a fling with you, I want to know everything there is to know about you. I want intimacy. With you," he said, his voice becoming increasingly husky.

"Gabe I'm confident, but I don't know if I'm that self-assured," she admitted.

"Sure, you are Annie. There is simply no one that comes even close. Please, Annie, when I was singing that tune earlier, I meant ever single word, I'm on the edge, and I'm falling, and it's a long way down," he said as he pulled her toward him.

Annie looked deeply into his eyes and saw that he was telling her the truth, and that he felt equally vulnerable in this moment. She pulled his head down for a kiss and said, "Alright cowboy, I guess I'm willing to see where this rodeo takes us." And their kiss felt like a promise, a butterfly emerging from the safety of its cocoon, fragile, new, vulnerable, not yet ready to take flight, still in stasis.

CHAPTER 18

"Sis! It's so good to see you. I don't have to ask how the trip went, you look radiant," Annie said.

"It was truly magical. To unplug for a whole month was such a luxury. I wish everyone had the opportunity to do it. There would sure be less angry people in the world," Darcy said.

"Sam, was Italy everything you remembered it to be?" Annie asked.

"And then some. It didn't hurt to have this babe by my side."

"I really missed you guys. I can't wait to see all of your pictures."

"I think we're going to invite some folks over to my place for a cookout and show everyone the photographs and catch up," Sam said.

"I'm in," Annie said.

Darcy noticing a certain glow about her sister asked, "Anything new with you?"

"Oh, you know, the usual."

"Really? As in all work?"

"Pretty much. I have managed to go out a few times," Annie said.

"As in 'date' go out?" Darcy said.

"Maybe."

"Anymore harassment from Bradley?"

"We'll talk about that later. Don't ruin my excitement over seeing you again," Annie said.

"You're right. We'll catch up on everything later. You are spending the night tonight, aren't you?"

"Of course," Annie said.

"Damn! Suddenly I realized I won't be with my woman 24/7," Sam said. "That is going to hurt like hell!"

Darcy glanced at Sam in the back seat, and a moment of reverence and love passed between them, "It will certainly take some getting used to for sure," Darcy said.

"Rather than getting used to it, we'll have to do something about that, won't we?" Sam said.

Darcy laughed then said, "The logistical nightmare, two thirty-somethings entrenched in their respective homes, trying to combine lives!"

"Be positive," Sam said.

"I am a realist at heart, you know that about me," Darcy replied.

"That's why I'm so good for you."

"You are good for me Sam Parker."

"Thank God we are here! I am suffocating with the schmaltz," Annie said, as she turned down the lane leading to the farm.

As soon as they arrived Slim came out to greet them, as if he'd been hiding in wait.

"Gall dern, it's about time ya'll got back," Slim said, looking almost cheerful.

Mimi and Bella barked ecstatically, and then Gabe rounded the corner and jogged the rest of the way to give Sam a big bear hug. "It's about time!" Gabe said. Then his eyes immediately found Annie's and they exchanged meaningful glances.

Darcy not one to miss much of anything couldn't resist asking, "So have you two been able to support each other in our long absence?"

Annie blushed slightly and Gabe was quick to respond with, "Me and your sister might have a little something going."

"I knew it!" Darcy said punching Sam lightly on the arm. "I called it."

"That she did," Sam said.

Gabe walked over to Annie and leaned down to touch her lips lightly with his own. "She kinda made it easy to forget I was carrying more responsibility."

"Looks like the barn didn't burn down in my absence so apparently not too much distraction," Sam said.

Cal approached and Gabe introduced him. "This is our new hire, Cal. Cal your real boss, the one who signs the paychecks, Sam and his fiancée Darcy."

"Hey, I feel like I already know ya," Cal said.

"Welcome to Parker Farm," Sam said, as he shook Cal's hand.

"No mistaking you two for sisters," Cal said as way of greeting Darcy.

Laughing Gabe said, "Ya think?"

"Wow is about all I got to say!" Cal said.

"Don't we know it!" Gabe said.

Closing the car door after Darcy was buckled in, Sam grabbed his duffle bag and hoisted it over his shoulder, "Shamrock, I'm going to miss waking up to your freckles every morning."

"You're going to make me cry," Darcy said, tearing up.

"It won't be long before we're cohabitating, if I have any say about it. Gabe let's plan on meeting tomorrow around nine am to go over everything. I don't start seeing patients until Monday, thank God!"

"See ya then chief. Get some rest," Gabe said.

"I love you Darcy Morgan." Sam said.

Eyes brimming with tears, Darcy said, "I love you too. Call me later...after your nap. Thanks for everything."

"Ciao amore mio."

∾

Driving away from the farm both women were quiet, with Darcy struggling to contain her tears and feeling completely adrift upon leaving Sam, and Annie having her own emotional reactions to the growing feelings she had for Gabe.

After a few miles Annie said, "Aren't we a pair?"

"I know, right?" Sniffling Darcy said, "I know it may not look like it, but I'm so incredibly happy right now. After Ryan was killed, I thought I'd never love again, and now, I love Sam so completely, it's like the old cliché, he makes me whole again."

"You two were meant to be. When I look at you together, it makes me want the same for myself. I won't settle for anything less. It's really beautiful to watch you two love each other."

"You will find that kind of love Annie, I'm sure of it."

"Darcy, things are moving so fast with Gabe. I really like him. It scares me because of his lifestyle. The music, the gigs, beautiful women at his beck and call, I feel so vulnerable."

"When we love we are vulnerable. It's a fact. It doesn't matter whether they work in an office as an accountant or as a musician, relationships are built on trust. You'll know what you need to know when you need to know it. The most important person you need to trust is yourself," Darcy said.

"It's hard for me to tell what the truth is sometimes. I lost touch with that inner voice for a while. After losing my way with Bradley, my ability to discern his twisted reality from what I knew to be true became difficult. If I said one thing, he would contradict it and tell me I was wrong and that I was the crazy one."

"God I could kill that man! It makes me so angry when I think of how he treated you! Classic verbal abuse: control and define someone, put them on the defensive, tell them what they are thinking and feeling despite protests to the contrary, the Bradley playbook," Darcy said.

"I'm so much stronger now. My life is really good, I'm happy, content with my career, my friendships, I didn't want the complication of a man in my life...and yet I already feel like it's too late to turn back now."

"If it helps ease your mind, Sam loves Gabe, he respects him and sees himself as somewhat of an older brother to Gabe. He trusts him a hundred percent," Darcy said.

Annie smiled at her sister, "Actually that does help a lot."

"I'm glad. I really like him Annie, and he obviously has it bad for you."

"Really? How could you tell?"

Annie's eagerness touched Darcy. "Puleeze! He couldn't take his eyes off you and they were smoldering. Very intense."

"I guess only time will tell," Annie said.

"Yep, we wouldn't want to skip to the last chapter anyhow, would we? That would spoil the story."

Annie laughed already feeling lighter from her talk with her sister. Darcy always made her feel like everything was going to be alright. "I am so glad you are home sis."

"It's good to be home. The trip was fabulous, but I like my life here, I'll be glad to settle back into it."

"The dogs are going to go crazy when they see you," Annie said.

"Can't wait."

"Here we are now."

CHAPTER 19

*S*haking his head in dismay, Gabe secured the latch he had discovered left open. That kind of a mistake on a horse farm could have disastrous consequences. He hated to think about what might have happened had Midnight discovered it first.

Everyone could make a mistake now and then, shit happens, it seemed like he was stumbling upon quite a few around the barn recently. Yesterday he found a flake of moldy hay in Midnight's stall, which could have caused her to colic or could even lead to respiratory problems or heaves.

He had taken Cal and Slim to the stall and showed them the mold and asked that they check every bale of hay they had left. He couldn't contain his outrage and had snapped, "This is horse care one-oh-one, if you fuck up like this again, I'm going to have to let you both go. These animals are dependent on us, their lives rest on our shoulders, this is unacceptable."

Slim had hung his head while Cal looked Gabe in the eye and said, "It won't happen again Gabe. We'll get right on checking the rest of our inventory for mold."

"I hain't seen no mold," was all Slim had said, as he left the stall.

Today it was the latch, yesterday the moldy hay, last week the water troughs, whiskey bottle, and cigarette butts. What the hell was going on around here? At least there had been no other signs of contaminated hay. Even so he had instructed them to thoroughly check every flake they put out from now on.

He glanced at his watch and realized it was time to meet with Sam. After that he planned on working with Midnight for a couple of hours. She was progressing in leaps and bounds and he was proud of how much she was prevailing over her fears. He knew she was going to come around, he could sense it. She was healing.

As he walked across the gravel drive heading for the office, a police cruiser pulled up next to him. The officer got out of his vehicle and approached Gabe.

"Is there something I can help ya with?" Gabe asked.

"Is this your farm?"

"I'm the manager."

"Got any ID on you?"

"Now why would I go around doing my barn chores carrying an ID with me?" Gabe said.

"I'd like to see some identification."

"What's this about?"

"I was dispatched here to do a wellness check," the officer said.

"Oh yeah, by who? Wait one minute here, who called you?" Gabe said.

"I'm not at liberty to divulge that information."

"Maybe not but you can divulge your name and your badge number."

"Do you have an elderly housebound woman living on the property?"

"No, nobody here fits that description," Gabe said.

"What's the address number here?" the officer asked.

"Sixty-six eighty."

The officer glanced down at his note pad and said, "Oh excuse me, I'm off by a couple of numbers."

"I still want your badge number," Gabe said.

"I'm sorry to have bothered you Mr. Hunter, have a nice day." The officer smiled and hopped back into his patrol car and left.

Sam showed up right as the cop drove away. "What was that all about?"

"Not sure, a 'wellness check' according to the cop."

"For who?"

"Dunno."

"Let's get started on this meeting. I'm staring down about twenty hours of catch up work," Sam said.

"Aren't vacations grand?" Gabe said. "Doesn't take long to lose that vacation glow does it?"

Much later it suddenly occurred to him that the officer had called him Mr. Hunter. Now how in the hell had he known that?

~

It was Saturday and Pepper had the day off and of course the priority was to ride her horse, Kizzy She passed Slim's trailer on the way out to the pasture where Kiz was grazing. He and Gabe were sitting on a lawn chairs concentrating on something they held in their hands. Laying curled up at Slim's feet was a little orange ball of fluff.

"A kitten!" Pepper said walking over to Slim and scooping him up. "What's his name?"

"Gus," Slim said.

"Aww, he is so cute. Watcha doing there?" Pepper asked, curious about the wooden figure in Slim's hand.

"Whittlin," Slim said.

"Whatcha whittling?"

"You sher are full of questions ain't cha?"

"Can I see?"

Slim held up a small wooden figurine of a horse. "Oh, Slim it's lovely! How did you do that with such a small piece of wood and that teeny tiny knife?"

"Jest like paring an apple."

"Hardly, this is hard as hell," Gabe said.

"Passed on to me from my paw. All the old-timers used ta whittle, nobody left doin it now," Slim said.

"That's why Slim agreed to teach me," Gabe said, standing up. "I guess I'd better get back to work."

"Jist keep a practicin' and it will come to ya before ya know it," Slim said.

"I'm afraid I'll need a few more lesson Slim."

"You know where ta find me I reckin."

"See ya around," Gabe said.

After Gabe left Pepper sat in the chair he had occupied.

"Slim, will you make something for me?" she asked.

"You want this here one you kin have it."

"Really? Yes, I would love to have it. Thank you."

He shoved it toward her, and she traded the kitten for the small wooden horse. "Is everything alright Slim?"

His eyes were faded and weary as he looked up at Pepper. "I reckin."

"You reckin?"

He smiled slightly, then said, "I'm gittin a little tired of being blamed for things I hain't done," he said.

"I'm sure nobody is blaming you for anything Slim— you're the best thing that ever happened to this ranch," Pepper said.

"Either I've done gone and lost it or someone else has, cuz there is a whole lotta of things going wrong around these parts."

"You can't take all the mistakes onto your own shoulders. Things seem to go wrong in streaks. Don't take it personal. I for one can't imagine how this place could go on without you."

"I always did like ya," Slim said.

"Thanks, Slim, it's mutual. Hang in there, tomorrow is a new day."

"It's a purty day fer a ride."

"That it is." Standing, Pepper said, "Thanks for the sculpture," and left to bring in Kizzy.

~

Gabe stroked Midnight's neck as he murmured soothing words to her, "How's my favorite filly? Hmm? You are doing great girl, you're so brave. Today we're going to go for a little ride in the outdoor arena. What do ya think of that?"

He placed the saddle pad on her back, and she turned to see what was there. So far so good. Then he placed the saddle on top which made her tense up. She blew out of her nostrils and her ears pricked up. "Easy now." She relaxed to Gabe's familiar voice.

"I'm going to put this here cinch around your belly. Real loose like," he talked to her as he reached under her belly to fasten the belt.

"That's good then..." He took his time tightening the cinch, a little at a time, until finally he felt it was secure enough for him to hop on. Gabe hadn't ridden her outside, nor had he had a saddle on her back until today. She seemed to be accepting of it so far. He would use the lunge line to warm her up before attempting to get on and ride.

After lunging Midnight for twenty minutes, Gabe was satisfied that she was in a relaxed frame of mind and decided it was time to get on. As he mounted her, she took a few quick steps then bolted at a full gallop, before he could even swing his leg all the way over, "Whoa!" Gabe quickly found his balance and brought her back to a walk, in short order. Her ears were pricked forward and her body was as tense as a guitar string strung too tight.

All of Gabe's focus was in that moment, at one with Midnight. He could feel every breath she took; he could feel her tight muscles bunched up beneath him, and knew he needed to distract her from the imaginary lions, tigers and bears. He used his legs and seat to get her attention. When her ears started to move forward and back, he knew she was finally with him.

"Good girl!"

At that moment Gabe looked up and finally noticed

that a small group had gathered at the fence line to watch. He nodded to them then returned all his attention back to the ride.

～

"That was so impressive!" Annie exclaimed. Reaching her hand towards Midnight, the horse blew into her palm her warm breath tickling her as she took the treat from Annie's hand. "You're a real beauty, aren't you girl? She's so soft." Turning to Gabe as she stroked Midnights neck, she said, "I don't think I have ever seen a more magnificent creature! I want her."

"Yeah, I'm fallin' for her, hook line and sinker myself," Gabe said. "I don't think she is in either of our budgets though."

"Wait, not only do I have to compete with groupies… now a horse too?" Annie said.

"Hain't all about you," Slim said. "You did good Gabe," Slim added.

"Thanks guys, but Midnight did all of the work," Gabe responded.

"She is something special that's for sure," Sam said.

Annie, still stinging from Slim's snarky comment, decided to pretend it didn't bother her. "Slim, Pepper showed me the wooden horse you made for her. You are so talented. Would you make one for me?"

"I reckin' I'm too busy fer that."

Gabe who had been unsaddling Midnight said, "Now Slim, the lady just paid you a compliment, is that any way to respond?"

Grumbling to himself Slim took his leave and Sam followed.

"Why does he hate me so much?" Annie asked.

"That's his way. He'll come around. Don't worry about it. If you'd like I can talk to him about it," Gabe offered.

"No, you can't force someone to like you. Forget it. I'll live."

"If you're sure. Come here you," Gabe said, pulling her into his arms. "I haven't given you a proper hello yet, have I? I'm no better than Slim."

"I'll forgive you this time," Annie said.

"What brings you to the farm on this beautiful spring day?"

"I got off work early and felt restless...so I thought I'd drop by and see you."

Gabe nuzzled her neck breathing in the floral and spice scent of her. He then nibbled on her ear lobe causing Annie to giggle. "That tickles!"

"How about dinner at my place tonight? We'll have a little fire in the fire pit...I may even serenade you with my guitar," Gabe said.

"That would be a yes," Annie said. "What time?"

"Six sound good to you?"

"I'll be here."

"Anything I should know about your eating preferences?" Gabe called out to her retreating back.

"Nope, I eat anything," Annie said as she climbed behind the wheel and took off.

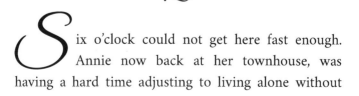

Six o'clock could not get here fast enough. Annie now back at her townhouse, was having a hard time adjusting to living alone without

Darcy's three mutts. The house felt empty and a little creepy. She still had shivers when she thought about her encounter here with Bradley. Surprisingly, there had been no fall out from running into Ike the other night. Maybe Bradley was finally moving on. She prayed that was true.

After slipping on a pair of black leggings with an oversized loose-fitting top, she studied her shoe selection. She opted for a pair of knee-high brown boots. She would take along a cardigan in case she got cool by the fire tonight.

She pulled her hair up into a ponytail, then after deciding to use eyeliner and shadow, at the last minute, went all out and added a dramatic red lipstick. Of course, she had chosen to wear her laciest and skimpiest lingerie. A girl had to feel good from the inside out, and tonight she was feeling sexy and beautiful.

She allowed herself time to stop and fill up the gas tank which was sitting on E as per usual. As she inserted the nozzle, a large gray truck pulled up to the pump on the other side of her. She didn't pay any attention until the driver gunned his motor causing the oversized truck to spew black smoke everywhere. She was thinking how rude the person was and why in the world did all these men think they needed Hummers and Hemi trucks, when the majority never used them to haul a damn thing.

"If it isn't my beautiful Annie. If I didn't know better, I would think that you were following me," Bradley said, laughing as he turned on the full charm.

Annie replied, "The real question is are you following me?"

"Paranoid much?"

"New truck?"

"As a matter of fact, it is."

"Just your style. I'm serious about this Bradley. This is another pretty big coincidence. I find it hard to believe that you just happened to need gas at this exact moment."

"These trucks are real gas guzzlers. Annie, when are you going to come to your senses and realize that we are meant to be?"

"You're beginning to freak me out."

"So, Ike tells me you're seeing some guy in a band. Gabe Hunter…good looking guy, apparently also into horses. Right up your ally isn't it?"

"How do you know he is into horses? More to the point, who I see is none of your business. Bradley this is your last chance and I mean it! Leave me alone and leave Gabe out of this mess," Annie said. She was equal parts angry and creeped out.

"Calm the fuck down! I stopped here to fill my tank, just like you. I can't help it that we had the same idea. You're starting to sound like a nut case Annie," Bradley said.

"Whatever. I'm not comfortable with you showing up at my workplace or my condo. And you just happen to be pulling in right behind me to fill up your tank? You need to back off."

Bradly replied, "Is that a threat?"

Annie stopped pumping her gas before she had even filled the tank so she could get the hell out of there as fast as possible. Putting her gas cap back on she didn't wait for a receipt before jumping back into her car.

As she closed her door Bradley called out to her, "It

was great running into you." Annie gunned her motor and sped away.

Bradley stood scowling as the car disappeared from his sight. Her sexy red lips and eye makeup hadn't escaped his notice. In his mind that could only mean one thing, she had a date with the fucking cowboy.

CHAPTER 20

Gabe was firing up the grill when Annie jumped out of her car and ran toward him, "Annie! What's wrong?" As he gathered her into his arms, he could feel her whole-body trembling as she cried.

"He is never going to leave me alone," Annie said between sobs.

"Whoa, slow down, it's okay babe, I'm here, who is never going to leave you alone?" He held her tight against him as he tried to figure out what was going on.

"My ex. I am so afraid he is never going to let me go," she said, then wiped her sleeve across her nose sniffling.

"What's he doing?"

"He turns up everywhere."

"Is he threatening you? We can call the police."

Annie laughed derisively, "He *is* the police."

"What? Your ex is a cop? Let's go inside and talk this through. Get your nerves calmed down a little, and decide what, if anything, needs to be done," Gabe said.

They sat in Gabe's tiny living room, with Annie snuggled up on his lap. She gave him a summary of what had led up to the initial breakup, control, jealousy, anger issues, then the back and forth, breaking up and reconciling, then the final break which Bradley refused to accept.

"He has shown up at my salon, I've seen him patrolling by my neighborhood, he confronted me when I was house sitting for Darcy because I hadn't been home and he didn't know where I was…"

"This guy sounds obsessed," Gabe said.

"The other night when I went to hear you play, his partner and bestie, Ike, was there, and I knew he would report back to Bradley immediately. Ike was asking me questions about you; he saw us together between sets. I'm sure that got Bradley fired up."

"I don't care if he's a cop, he's not above the law," Gabe said.

"I just told him that he needed to back off."

"Maybe I should pay him a visit myself. Man to man," Gabe said hugging her tighter.

"No! That would be a terrible idea. I'm alright now. I feel much calmer." Placing her palm on Gabe's toned stomach she said, "I think I heard your stomach growling, let's get supper started."

"If you're sure about this. Look I don't know the guy, but he sounds like a real piece of work. I'm not trying to scare you but stay alert."

"You know, it really isn't anything new, but it's so stressful running into him. Maybe he was telling me the truth and just happened to be getting gas at the same time. Coincidences do happen."

"Maybe it was, but I seriously doubt it," Gabe said.

"I'm ready to change the subject. Just hold me."

"You sure do feel good in my arms."

"Yeah."

Gabe leaned down to taste her lips. "I like the red," he said as he nipped lightly on her bottom lip.

She put her arms around his neck and held his head as she slipped her tongue into Gabe's parted lips.

He sucked in his breath and hungrily took what she was offering. His mouth covered hers as he cradled her face between his hands. He swung his legs up onto the couch bringing her with him so that they were now both lying down with her on top of him.

She straddled him, her thin leggings not much of a barrier between his erection and her wet center. He moaned as she rubbed herself against him back and forth, riding him through the barrier of their clothing. He reached under her top to fondle her breasts through her bra. With both hands massaging her breasts he began to tease her nipples, pinching and pulling on the erect buds until she arched back without inhibition. Riding him harder, she rubbed against his manhood in primal lust. Her head, thrown back, exposed the creamy skin of her throat. Gabe was mesmerized by her complete abandon.

Pulling her down toward his chest he flipped her over so that he was now on top. With shaky hands he unbuttoned her top to expose voluptuous breasts ripe and ready to burst from the confines of the lacey silk bra.

He wanted to take her like a wild beast. Mate like the animals that they were. He plundered her mouth then kissed his way to her breast, pulling aside the lace to feel her bare skin against his lips. Putting his open mouth on her nipple he used his tongue to circle it, before gently pulling it into his mouth. He suckled like he was drinking her nectar, tugging and pulling harder until she cried out.

"Gabe, take me!"

Gabe looked at her flushed cheeks, her luscious lips, her lush hair now freed from the ponytail and fanning out like a halo around her face, and knew he was lost. "Hold on, let me go get a condom," he said, reluctantly leaving her.

Gabe returned and Annie watched as he pulled his tee-shirt over his head, appreciating his defined arm muscles as they flexed, his ripped six-pack abs, the way his dark hair peeked out above his low-slung jeans.

"Gabe, I need you now!"

He quickly unzipped his jeans and pulled them off and stood in his boxer briefs memorizing every detail of this beauty gazing up at him with such fierce desire. And it was all for him.

"I've never wanted any woman as much as I want you." He peeled off the last remaining barrier of his clothing to expose his erect penis. Kneeling beside the couch he began to undress Annie. He removed her shirt, then unclasped her bra and pulled it off, his breath hitched at the sight of her. Perfection. Her full breasts, the pink rose color of her nipples, now erect with passion, pleased his senses and almost drove him over the edge with desire. He took in a deep long breath to pace himself; he didn't want to rush things and blow it. Their first time was going to be special.

His warm hands splayed her waist as he grasped the elastic waist band and gently drug her leggings down her long shapely thighs. He put his lips on her flat belly and nuzzled, then kissed her mound through the silky panties. Her musky smell with a hint of floral scent practically drove him crazy. He tugged them off and tossing them onto the heap of clothing already on the floor.

Still kneeling beside her, he parted her legs further and fondled her clitoris with his thumb as he inserted a finger into her vagina. Capturing her nipple with his lips he began seductively and rhythmically sucking as he repeatedly plunged his finger into her moist warm womanhood. She writhed under his expert lovemaking. Lifting his gaze, their eyes met, and he knew she was ready.

He mounted her as she spread her legs wide to receive him. His buttocks clenched as he thrust deeply into her and began to pump, slowly at first, then harder and faster as she urged him on.

Sweat glistening on his brow, arms taut as he held himself above her, at last he reached his threshold and exploded in orgasm. It rocked him to his core and seemed to go on for eternity. He was barely conscious of Annie calling out his name as she gasped and convulsed beneath him as he lost himself inside of her. She grasped his hair, as she cried out with a final shuddering breath of release.

Limbs intertwined, they laid together, both engulfed in their post-coital passion. Annie was the first to break the silence.

"Gabe?"

"Yeah?"

"That was amazing," she said.

"Honestly, I am shattered," Gabe said, only half joking.

"You are an incredible lover Gabe."

"And you are breathtaking!" he replied. Gabe propped up on his elbow to look intently into her eyes. Satisfied with the sexual fulfillment reflected there he stroked her cheek with his thumb and said, "Not to change the subject, but should I try firing up the grill again?"

"Yes."

Trailing kisses across her breasts he said, "I hate to leave your delicious body."

Annie, already becoming aroused again said, "If you don't start the grill now you may as well forget it."

Annie stroked his bare shoulders and back, turned on by the sensuousness of skin on skin where their naked bodies touched. *Soft and hard.* Gabe suckled her nipple then raised his head, eyes hooded and dark with desire, which made her feel feminine and beautiful. Brushing his hair back from his brow she cradled his head against her breast as he continued his skillful mastery.

"Yes," Annie said squirming beneath him.

"Baby, I will never get enough of you," Gabe said moving up to her lips. There was nothing gentle about this kiss. This was an insatiable hunger desperate for repletion. He was taking, demanding that she surrender to him. He spread her lips wide with his tongue as he ravished her mouth. He pulled her tongue deep inside and suckled. Only to then thrust his own back into her mouth. He rubbed his hard shaft against her soft belly as she opened her thighs wide then wrapped them around him.

Gabe grabbed another condom from the end table and quickly slipped it on, entering her like a man possessed. Watching her face, eyes closed, her teeth biting her lower lip as she sought release, he rode her hard. She moaned with ecstasy, her large breasts bouncing with each thrust. She had the most beautiful breasts he had ever seen. Her nipples were perfect. The color of a pink rose bud, large and ripe for suckling. Her breasts were full and round like two perfect melons. As she began to come, he held his pelvis tight against hers, stilling his movements. He watched as wave after wave overtook her. He thrust one more time then shuddered and was lost as he orgasmed inside of her.

They both laid there unable to move, utterly spent. The room had become dark with the setting of the sun. They listened to each other breathe and felt the rise and fall of their ribs, Gabe still resting on top of Annie. His penis was still inside of Annie and she didn't move for fear of it slipping out, she was not ready to let him go. She loved the feeling of him resting there. She didn't think she could move even if she wanted to.

"Annie?"

"Yes."

"Should I try firing up the grill again?"

"I guess I'll let you go this time," she said, smiling in the dark.

"Annie?"

"Yes?"

"I don't want to let you go," he said.

"Alright, I'll come with you," Annie said.

"I was hoping you'd say that."

CHAPTER 21

*M*uch later, after their dinner had been cooked and consumed, Gabe gathered some wood and kindling for the campfire. The air had turned cooler, so Annie donned her jacket and a borrowed knit hat from Gabe. There was a circle of logs and a few tree stumps around the fire-pit to sit on. Annie chose a log big enough for both of them and watched him dexterously bring the twigs and branches to a roaring blaze.

She noticed the flames casting light and shadow over his handsome face, making his expression seem mysterious and inscrutable. She suddenly felt lonely and needed his warmth, "Are you almost done?"

"Why, are you missing me?"

"How'd you guess?"

Gabe put his stick down and went to gather Annie up in his arms. "Cuz I was feeling it too." He leaned in for a deep kiss.

"Are you going to play for me?" Annie asked.

"Sure, if you want me too."

"That would be a yes," Annie said.

Gabe turned and grabbed his guitar that he'd leaned up against a stump beside him and began to tune it. As he strummed, she thought his forearms and hands were the sexiest thing she had ever seen. Large, tanned, strong and muscular, she knew she would never be able to erase the feel of their prowess on her body.

He began to strum his guitar and softly sing a Bret Young song, *In Case You Didn't Know*. As he sang for her he looked deeply into her eyes, and she was lost. The song melted her heart. He sang about how crazy he was about her, that he couldn't live without her. Telling her everything he'd been feeling but hadn't been able to say.

"Gabe, that was so beautiful, thank you."

"That song could have been written for you, by me, I meant every single word, Annie." He sat his guitar back down and put his arm across her shoulders. Annie looked up at the full moon and sighed with contentment.

Hearing a barred owl in the distance, the night took on a mystical quality. The crackling fire, the hooting owl, the glorious moon, a gorgeous man serenading her, what the hell, this was probably the most perfect night of Annie's entire life. "It honestly feels like we are the only two on the planet right now," she said. He dipped his head and kissed her neck. The atmosphere between them went from searing hot to heat-stroke level in a split second.

He tucked her hair behind her ear and rolled her bottom lip with his thumb. She drew it into her mouth and bit down softly.

"You in that hat..." He lightly grasped her chin and

pulled her head toward his tipping it back as he leaned down for a kiss. "You taste so damn good! Mmm," he said against her lips. "Annie girl will you put me out of my misery and spend the night with me?"

"Yes, I'd like that."

"Like?"

"Gabe Hunter, if I don't get to spend the night tonight, I will curl up and die, right here on the spot. Is that better?"

"Much." He grinned at Annie from ear to ear. "You realize that I only have a twin sized bed, don't you?"

"All the better," Annie said.

"I was hoping you'd feel that way. Before we head in how about some smores?"

She pulled away and said, "You're kidding me, right? I love smores."

"I'll be right back," he jumped up and ran to the house, returning shortly with marshmallows, graham crackers, and chocolate.

Licking the last of the melted chocolate from her fingers, Annie said, "This reminds me of camping with my dad. We always had smores after we returned from star gazing."

"We had a lot of nights sitting around a campfire at my grandma and gramps' farm," Gabe shared. "Smores were always on the menu."

Yawning Annie said, "Are you ready to turn in? I'm starting to feel sleepy."

"Yeah that twin bed and lying down next to you is calling to me. You can go on in and get into the bathroom first while I make sure the fire is completely out. There is a new toothbrush in the hall closet for ya, and towels and washcloths."

"Thanks. Hurry up, I'll miss you," Annie said.

~

They crawled under the covers and spooned with Annie's back snuggled up against Gabe's chest and his arms around her. He buried his nose in her hair and drank in the feminine scent of her.

"How come you always smell so damn good?"

"I do?" she answered sleepily.

"Yeah, you just about drive me crazy."

Annie yawned again and already half asleep said, "I'm so sleepy."

"Go to sleep babe, I'll be right behind you." She didn't even hear him; she was already out.

~

The first thing Annie noticed upon awakening was Gabe's arms around her with his hand under her tee-shirt cupping her bare breast. The next thing she felt was his erection pressing into her behind. She wiggled her buttocks against him snuggling up against his hard shaft.

"Good morning," Gabe said groggily.

Annie turned over in bed to face him, and put her full lips against his, lingering there, but not really kissing him. He opened one eye and peered at her through his lashes. She reached down to rub his erection through his boxers as he groaned. "Is this for me?" Annie asked.

"There is nobody but you," Gabe said.

"I'll bet you've said that a time or two."

"Nope this is a first," Gabe said.

"Swear?"

"Swear."

"Roll back over," Gabe said.

Annie complied and once again had her back to Gabe. He pulled her tee-shirt off and threw it aside then pulled her panties down and pushed his penis between her thighs from behind, rubbing his shaft against her as she held on to him from the front creating more friction. He kissed her shoulder at the curve of her neck and felt her shudder. Her skin was like silk.

He teased her nipples with one hand and stimulated her clitoris with the other, all the while thrusting in and out on the surface without penetrating. He quickly grabbed a condom because he knew he was close to climaxing and just as he entered her vagina from behind Annie erupted. He continued to stimulate her in the front as he rode her from behind. He moved his hands to hold her steady as he passionately plunged harder and deeper to reach his own climax.

"Oh baby, you feel so damn good," Gabe murmured into her hair.

She turned to face him again and put her arms around his neck pulling him in for a long sensuous kiss. "Gabe, you're like a drug I don't think I can quit, it scares the crap out of me," she admitted.

"I don't want you to quit…ever. I'll happily be your addiction," Gabe said.

"You say that now, but what about the nights you play music and all of the beautiful women are throwing themselves at you, what then?"

"Same. I told you before, one-night stands are lonely and boring. It's not what I want."

"Gabe, I want to believe you, I do, but it won't be all that easy, temptation can't always be contained."

"I won't be tempted, that's the thing, I only want you."

"We'll just have to cross that bridge when we come to it," Annie said.

"We won't come to it Annie," Gabe said firmly.

"I hear you. I want to believe."

"Have a little faith."

"I'll try."

"On to more practical matters, let me fix you some breakfast, I'm sure you have things to do today," Gabe offered.

"Breakfast is my favorite meal."

"Good to know, sunshine."

She watched his muscular backside as he put his boxers back on and walked out of the bedroom. His strong glutes and hamstrings were solid. His back was ripped as well. She could see the muscular definition of his lats and trapezius muscles, and the deltoids and triceps of his arms.

She had never been as sexually aroused by a man as she was by Gabe. She hadn't been kidding when she said she was hooked. What the hell, it was too late to turn back now. She may as well enjoy the ride for as long as it lasted. Climbing out of bed she pulled her tee back on and followed him out to the kitchen.

She sat on a stool and watched him whisk some batter in a bowl as the griddle heated up. "Are you making pancakes for me?"

Grinning as he poured the batter onto the sizzling hot griddle he replied, "Yep, just for you."

"I'm crazy about you Gabe Hunter," Annie said softly.

His whole body became still. He stared at Annie with an intensity filled with longing and hope. Annie got up from the stool and came up behind Gabe wrapping her arms around him. Resting her cheek against his bare back she said, "How could I not be?"

He flipped the flapjacks and said, "Great timing honey girl, if you want burnt pancakes."

Her lips curled up against his skin then she kissed his back and said, "I'm going to wash my hands, I'll be right back."

She looked around at Gabe's décor as she made her way to the bathroom and had to smile. Absolutely no feminine touches anywhere. All guy. No frills, no knickknacks, no photos, bare bones. Sitting on the back of the commode was a tiny parched plant that was on its last leg. She hadn't noticed it the night before. She picked up the pathetic greenery and suddenly got the giggles. The more she looked at it the more she laughed.

Walking back to the kitchen holding her belly with one hand and the plant in the other, by this time practically howling with mirth said, "Gabe your one attempt at domestication has resulted in the murder of an innocent victim. I enter into evidence the philodendron." She held it up for Gabe to see and after a sheepish look he joined in in the merriment.

Watching her radiant face alight with laughter stirred him, "What you don't think I have a good aesthetic sensibility?" He took the plant out of her hands and pulled her against him hugging her tightly in his arms.

"I'm crazy about you too," he said, then lowered his

head to kiss her. The kiss was gentle almost reverent. "God Annie, I'm falling for you."

"Kiss me again Gabe," she said, suddenly overcome with a need that felt like an unquenchable thirst. It would never be enough, it would never grow old, and this man was the only one who could satisfy her. Her lips clung to his and she drank of him.

He gently pulled away and went to plate their breakfast. Gabe sat hers down in front of her and when she saw the face created with canned whipped cream, two eyes, a nose, and smile, she was so touched that she felt tears spring to her eyes.

Seeing her brimming eyes Gabe said, "Baby, don't you like my artwork?"

"It is the sweetest thing a guy has ever done for me."

"That is a damn shame. You deserve the world Annie; you deserve to be cherished every single day of your life."

"Now I don't want to eat him."

Gabe used his fork to scramble the face, so it was now just a white blob of cream. "Is that better?"

She smiled at him through her tears and his heart melted even more. He watched her expectantly as she took her first bite. "Well?"

"Mmmm."

He kissed a smidgen of cream from her upper lip then dug into his own stack of cakes. "Oh yeah that's what I'm saying. What I lack in interior design I make up for in culinary skill."

"Brag much?"

"Not much."

"Good to know."

"I don't want you to go," Gabe said.

"Me either."

"When can I see you again?"

"Tonight."

"Really? *Yes!*" he threw his fist up in the air cracking Annie up. "Now I think I will survive."

"My place or yours?" he asked.

"Here."

"Good."

"Just pack your bags and stay awhile."

"Pretty tempting. I may pack enough for a couple of nights," she said.

"That would mean a lot to me," Gabe said, earnestly.

"I need to get my butt in gear and get out of here," Annie said after rinsing off her plate.

"I'll see you tonight," Gabe said.

"Thank you for everything, I have never felt so taken care of in my entire life."

"You make it easy."

"Bye Gabe."

"Bye Annie, see you tonight. Don't worry about eating before you get here. I'll have something for us, maybe Chinese takeout."

Annie gave him a quick kiss before heading out the door, "Sounds good to me."

CHAPTER 22

"Can we keep this on the down-low?" Darcy asked Captain Robert Gregory, an old friend from her days on the force.

"Of course, what's up?" he asked.

"I understand her reasons, but I feel like my sister is making a mistake in not reporting this to you, so I am going behind her back."

"Is this about Bradley?"

"Yes."

"Have a seat. Would you like some coffee?" he asked.

"Sure."

Captain Gregory poured them each a cup and sat down behind his desk with a deep frown on his face. "Talk to me."

"I just got back from a month away and after the conversation I had with Annie today, I'm very concerned for her safety. I feel like he has crossed a line. He keeps showing up…at a gas station, at her condo, at her salon, always the same sad song, "I love you; I want you back, I'm a changed man"... the problem is that he won't take no for an answer."

"Darcy, there is hardly a law against heartbreak."

"I know all of this sounds lame when I say it out loud, but Annie had the distinct impression that he had been inside her condo, nothing she could prove, but things were moved around, back door unlocked, stuff like that," Darcy said.

"Again, not much we can do about somebody's suspicions, unless she wants to file a restraining order, but that's complicated too. The threat is implied but there has been no physical violence so it's her word against his at this point."

"I know that, and she doesn't want to jeopardize his job. She is not even sure that some of it isn't just coincidence, but she feels he is getting more obsessive and that her reentering the dating world might have tripped his trigger."

"What would you like me to do?"

"Is there any way you could say something to him off the record? Just to let him know that you are aware of the situation and have your eyes on him. It might be enough to wake him up and make him back off my sister. She is getting increasingly uncomfortable with these random encounters."

"There is always the danger that it could backfire."

"I've thought of that, but I think he's basically a coward, so I would place odds that he'd scurry for cover, like the rat that he is," Darcy said.

"Look, I'll see what I can do as a favor to you, you know he is not my favorite officer to begin with."

"I knew I could count on you Bob, and I hate having to ask."

"Consider it done. There is no guarantee on how he'll respond but, I must agree with you, he is likely to back off if an authority steps in. Afterall, he is a classic bully."

"Thank you so much, I won't forget this."

"Patty and I would love to have you over for dinner sometime soon. You can bring that fiancée of yours as well. We'd like to meet him,"

"Sounds lovely. You'll love Sam." Darcy said, her soft expression telling the captain all he needed to know.

"I'm happy for you Darcy."

"Thanks Captain. Have Patty give me a call and we'll get something in the book."

Rising from his seat, he walked around to give Darcy a brief hug, "Sounds good, we'll see you soon then."

"Yep, and thanks again, I feel like a thousand pounds is off my shoulders."

"Glad I could help. We'll have to see how it all plays out. Hopefully this will be the end of it."

Darcy held up her hand with her fingers crossed. "Bye Bob."

"See ya soon," he replied, thoughtful as he watched her leave his office. She'd been through enough crazy shit in her life, he would do anything he could to protect her from any further pain or loss.

⁓

"You did what?" Annie said, eyes wide with panic.

"He will handle it with care, he is my friend." Darcy said reassuringly.

"Oh my God! I hope you're right."

"Listen Annie, you're running out of options. Short of a restraining order I think this is the best one."

"So, he is just going to say something friend-to-friend like?"

"Yes, just a friendly warning, letting him know that he is aware of what's been going on…trust me he will do it skillfully."

"I wish you would have asked me first, but I think it could work," Annie said coming around to the idea.

"Me too."

"I'll be staying over at Gabe's for the next night or two."

"Sounds like you've taken it to the next level."

"I'm crazy about him. Honestly sis, I think I am falling in love," Annie said.

"I have no advice; the heart wants what the heart wants. I know all about that."

"It's so much more than his killer body, he's funny, and he can go deep, ya know? He is all about intimacy, listening, sharing from the heart, I've never had anything like this with a man before."

"I'm so happy for you."

"It's all moving so fast, I would be lying if I said I wasn't afraid, but fortunately I've had the best role model for walking toward fear and kicking it's gnarly ass, and I'm looking at her." Annie said getting up to give her big sister a hug.

Darcy, still seated, hugged her little sister back and said, "As the saying goes…love ain't for sissies."

"Not to change the subject, but how does next weekend sound for a gathering to show our pictures from the trip?" Darcy asked.

"Lovely. Anything I can do to help?"

"Nope, just show up and bring your man."

"As long as he doesn't have a gig, I'm sure he'll be down for it."

"We can do either night, so check with him and I'll wait to hear if one night works better than another. I have to see you two in action."

"Great, under the microscope, fun times," Annie said.

"I'll be circumspect."

Laughing Annie replied, "Yeah right. Unfortunately, I've got to go, but thanks for talking with the captain, I think."

"You're welcome. See you later. Have fun tonight."

"I intend to."

CHAPTER 23

fter eating their spring rolls and Lo Mein, Gabe got up and rinsed off their plates. "I have something I want to show you. Are you up for a drive?" Gabe asked.

"Yes, what is it?"

"Not telling," he replied.

"Hmm so mysterious, it's got me guessing."

"You won't have to wait long, its right around the corner," Gabe said.

In less than two minutes they pulled down a long drive leading to an old white brick farmhouse. There was a small barn that appeared to go with the property and a for sale by owner sign in the yard.

"Well, what do you think?"

"It's big, and looks like it could use a little TLC, but it has loads of potential," Annie said.

"That's what I thought. I'm thinking of putting in an offer."

"Wow! That's a big step."

"I've been looking for a while, but not too seriously. I've been comfortable where I'm at. It suits the single life. But this property is close to work, Slim could have my place, and I'd have a place to call home. You and me would have more privacy."

Her heart skipped a beat. *Did he just imply what I think he did?* Said so casually, but it definitely fell under the heading of future talk. She didn't know what to say.

"It's important to me that you like it."

"Let's go peek inside the windows," Annie said.

"I'll go one better. I know the seller and he told me I could take you through it anytime. I've got a key," he said holding it up and grinning.

They entered through the side door which led into a mud room right off the large eat-in kitchen. Annie peered into the dining/living room and gasped at the stone fireplace that encompassed much of the living room wall. It was a stunning focal point with the simple wood mantel mirroring old wooden beams overhead. The ceilings were high, and the floors were hardwood that someone had painstakingly refinished.

"Wow! There is so much natural light, and that fireplace…" Annie said. "Is it functional?"

"Yep. A full bath downstairs and one on the second floor. One bedroom down and two upstairs. I know it's a lot of space for a single person, but…"

"It's fabulous Gabe. I'm excited for you," Annie said.

"I'm glad you like it Annie. It needs some work, but I like fixing up things and working with my hands."

"You could certainly live in it while you make the improvements over time."

"I'm hoping you'll help me with paint color and furnishings, I'll need your expertise."

"I would love that. We'll have to make your bathroom plant a focal point," she said, not being able to resist the gentle teasing about his forsaken house plant.

"You had to get that in didn't you," he grabbed her into his arms and tickled her as she shrieked.

"I give! I'm sorry, your little plant is so lucky to have you," she said giggling as she wiggled out of his arms. "Race you upstairs," she called over her shoulder as she ran upstairs.

He was right on her heels and they were both breathless when they reached the top landing. Gabe pulled her to him again but this time it was to steal a kiss.

"Come here you vixen," he said.

She looked up at him seductively, "Who are you calling a vixen, cowboy?"

He kissed her deeply and they were lost in a swirl of desire. Gabe pinned her against the wall and fondled her breast through her clothing. She groaned as he pinched her nipple and felt an immediate warmth spreading between her thighs. She rubbed his erection through his jeans, as he thrust his tongue deeper.

He finally lifted his head, eyes burning with passion, he said raggedly, "I will never get enough of you."

Her eyes were glazed over and she was struggling to form a thought other than *take me now*. She traced his lips with her fingertip and then slipped it into his mouth. He sucked it gently. "Let's finish the tour and get back to my place," he said.

"Yes."

∾

A week later and Annie was still camped out at Gabe's. Two nights had turned into four, then six and now it was the weekend and they were getting ready to walk over to Sam's house for the party. Annie, still not dressed yet, sat in her bra and panties and watched as Gabe stepped out of the shower, handing him a towel to dry off with. She followed his movements, first drying his feet, then thighs with the soft downy hair, leading up to his pelvis and beautiful penis. She couldn't hold the tension any longer and reached for the towel saying, "Here let me finish."

Sitting on the only available seat in the tiny bathroom, the toilet, she reached between his thighs with the towel and gently dried him off, taking a little extra time to tease him by cupping him and massaging him with the towel. She reached further to dry between his gluteal cleft, causing him to groan.

"Turn around," she ordered.

He turned his back to her, and she had an eye-full of his glorious ass. She leaned in and kissed both cheeks, saying "Now you can't say I never kissed your ass."

She stood to reach his back and shoulders, planting little kisses along the way. She licked a few droplets from his skin, and he suddenly turned and grabbed her. His erection was full on and throbbing. He pressed into her as he plundered her mouth.

Annie pulled back, breathless. She held his penis and began to fondle him, gripping his shaft she slid her hand up and down his erection, simultaneously cupping and rolling his testicles in her other hand. He pulled her close, shuddering he climaxed.

"Babe."

Slipping out of her panties and bra, she stepped back into the shower with Gabe. "Deja Vu," she said.

He lathered his hands and slipped them between her legs, "Gabe we're going to be late," she said protesting, but not very convincingly.

"They can wait," he said.

She spread her legs and leaned against the shower wall as he worked his magic. The water cascaded down their bodies, as her open palms pressed into the tiles. Her knees were weak with desire as she felt the tension in her body build, longing for release. He sucked on her nipple, as he skillfully rubbed her clitoris inserting his finger at the same time.

Gabe raised his head to look up at Annie and caught his breath at her wanton abandon. He picked her up and thrust inside her as she wrapped her legs around his waist. His whole body strained toward her, all his back muscles taut, buttocks contracting, thighs engaged, his hands braced on either side of her as she clung to him. Just as he was ready to come, he pulled out as she climaxed with him.

"Annie girl, you have no idea." He covered her mouth with his.

She kissed him back.

"Shall we try this again?" Gabe said, playfully pulling on her earlobe.

"I'm not sure I have the strength, but I don't want to be the one to tell my sister we're not coming because we've screwed ourselves into a coma," she said, giggling at the thought.

"Um yeah, I don't think I want to be around for that conversation," he said, chuckling.

"Let's do this then," she said.

"I'm drying off all by myself this time," he said.

"Spoilsport, no sense of adventure."

They were only a half hour late and since it was ultra-casual, no big deal. Gabe immediately went to talk with Zane Dunn, his attorney and friend, to fill him in on the progress he was making with Midnight. Zane's wife Allie sat huddled in a corner holding their daughter Olivia and laughing with Sam's sister, Casey. Annie was surprised to see that Slim had shown up. He was sitting alone looking uncomfortable, so Annie braved the waters and walked over to him.

"Hey Slim,"

"Hey yerself."

"I'll bet you're glad Sam is back."

"I reckin I don't need no hand holdin," Slim replied.

"Who said you did?"

Pepper walked up and joined them relieving a little of the tension between the two. "I'm so glad you made it, Slim. I know this isn't your cup of tea," Pepper said sympathetically. Annie had to force her mouth from hanging open at the transformation in Slim. He simply beamed at the young woman.

What's she got that I don't have? "How's it going Pepper?" Annie asked.

"Pretty good. We haven't seen much of Gabe in the off hours lately, have we Slim?" She said teasing Annie.

"She done cast her spell I reckin," he said, grudgingly.

Indignant Annie said, "How do you know it wasn't him that cast a spell?"

"Look at him over yonder, he kin barely keep his eyeballs off ya." Nodding his head as if that proved his point.

Annie glanced over at Gabe and they exchanged a smile. Thinking of their shower together made Annie tingle between her thighs. She had to pull her eyes away to concentrate on the conversation with Slim and Pepper.

She had missed out on what they were saying, and Pepper laughed and said, "See Slim, I would say the spell goes both ways."

"I'm sorry, what were you saying?" Annie said, her cheeks turning pink.

"We was sayin that Midnight is comin' round," Slim repeated.

"I know. It's so exciting."

"Not to change the subject but Slim, what's this I hear that you're having some tests done at the hospital?" Pepper asked.

"Hain't nothin' just them greedy basturds tryin to get blood outta a turnip," he said.

"Sam said you haven't been feeling too good," Pepper said. "You know it's the nurse in me, I have to know what's going on with my friends."

"Jist old age, I'm slowin down," he admitted.

"Look me up when you're there, I can take you to lunch at the cafeteria, the food's not too bad," Pepper offered.

"You werkin Wednesday?"

"As a matter of fact, I am," Pepper said.

"I'll look ya up."

"I'm counting on it."

Gabe walked up and put his arm around Annie, tucking her up against his side. "Hey Slimbo, whatcha' got going?" Gabe said.

"Makin small talk, jist about my least favorite thing

to do," he grumbled.

"You know you love it, who are you kidding," Pepper said bumping Slim with her elbow.

Pepper received a small grin for her trouble which dumbfounded Annie yet again. She glanced up at Gabe to see if he noticed but apparently, he hadn't.

Just then Sam called for everyone's attention, "For those of you who haven't figured it out, this is a self-serve establishment. Help yourselves to munchies, beers are in the cooler, wine in the fridge, we'll set up the big screen TV and start the slide show shortly. Grab some grub then find a seat. Glad you all could make it. It's great to see everybody!"

Gabe and Annie sat on the floor against the wall, with Annie snuggled up between his legs, leaning back against his chest, his arms wrapped around her. Pepper and Slim had pulled up kitchen chairs and sat next to one another. After making sure everyone had beverages and food Darcy and Sam gave a little talk about their trip then took their seats and started the slide show.

Casey, Sam's sister, and her husband Charlie, had called the love seat. Allie sat on the floor at Zane's feet with Olivia happily sitting on Clare's lap. Olivia was adorable, chubby cheeks and legs, a happy baby with her front and bottom two teeth often on display because she was always smiling.

Annie noticed that Zane couldn't keep his hands off Allie. He always had to be touching her. Currently, he had his knees on either side of her and his hand in her hair. She leaned her head back in his lap to smile up at him and he leaned down and kissed her. Nice to know that spark didn't have to dry up after marriage and children.

Annie's favorite photograph was one that Sam took of Darcy throwing her coins into Trevi Fountain. "OMG! You did it. Was that your three coins or mine?" Annie asked.

"Yours, that's why I had Sam take the shot…just for you."

Gabe looked a little stunned, then murmured, "I had the same request, I asked Sam to throw coins in for me too."

"I remembered that you told him not to forget Trevi Fountain, I thought maybe it was a sign," Annie said.

Gabe nuzzled her neck, nibbling her skin, "And now?" he whispered.

"Now?"

"Do you still think it was a sign?"

"Yes."

"Me too."

Annie had never felt this level of connection, she honestly felt like he could be her soul mate…if there was such a thing. That terrified her. Did he feel the same she wondered?

After the last slide was shown everyone mingled for a while, catching up, telling stories, then Zane said he had an announcement to make.

"Everybody you are the first to know, Allie and I are expecting another baby!"

"Woohoo! That's great!" Sam said.

Sheepishly Allie said, "Full disclosure, you aren't exactly the first, I had to tell Casey, but Charlie, I made her swear that she wouldn't even tell you. We are thrilled beyond belief."

Allie and Zane glowed. Allie had never looked more beautiful or content and Zane hovered over her like

Tarzan protecting Jane. He was so tender and obviously devoted to her. It was like a storybook romance. Happy ending and all. It made Annie long for hers.

Annie and Gabe left holding hands, leisurely walking back to his house. The stars were shining brightly in the sky and they decided to sit outside his place for a few minutes before turning in.

"You know I should probably move back to my own place tomorrow since it's Sunday and we've both got killer weeks ahead of us," Annie said sounding melancholy.

"Don't leave me baby," Gabe coaxed.

"We have to get back to real life eventually."

"We have been, we've been working and functioning quite well, I thought anyway," Gabe said.

"I agree, we've been playing house well together, but we both have homes and responsibilities, we knew it wasn't going to last forever, we talked about three nights and it's been a week, which, by the way, has flown by."

"It's been the best week of my life Annie."

"Mine too." She sighed deeply, already feeling lonely.

Attempting to cheer her up Gabe said, "My plant is going to miss you."

She laughed then punched him lightly on the arm. "You're so bad."

"Let's make a date for Wednesday, seven o'clock dinner at my place," Gabe said.

"Small consolation but at least it's something," she said, sounding pitiful.

"We'll figure it out."

"I know, I'm just sad."

"Me too, babe."

CHAPTER 24

Midnight's spirits were improving in leaps and bounds. Gabe turned her out after a particularly successful training session and marveled at how good it felt to see her confidence build and how gratifying it was to be a part of her healing. He had earned her trust and in the process a partnership had been born.

He decided to catch up on some paperwork and surprised Slim who was behind Gabe's desk, looking like a kid caught in the cookie jar. "Watcha looking for Slim?"

Head down, Slim mumbled under his breath something Gabe couldn't quite make out about a grain order, but Gabe wasn't convinced. "You got something you'd like to talk about Slim?"

"Naw, sorry ifin I startled ya," he said. "I'll let ya git back to yer werk."

Gabe decided to let it go for now and said, "What time is your appointment tomorrow?"

"Prit near at sunrise."

"Good luck Slim. You don't have time to be sick, we need you around here," Gabe said, squeezing Slims bony shoulder.

"You got that there young buck werkin fer ya now, I'm gist an old worn out cowboy."

"You know that's not true. You aren't ready to be put out to pasture yet."

"Thanks fer that," Slim said, gifting Gabe with a rare smile.

"I mean it. I don't think I could manage the place without you."

"I'll try to not let ya down."

"Keep me posted."

"Fer sure."

After he left, Gabe tried sleuthing out what Slim had been searching for. It appeared that he had been in his side drawer because it wasn't closed all the way. Pulling it open there was a folder not completely tucked in. Gabe grabbed it and saw that it was his employment applications file. Not a very thick one at that. Why the hell would Slim be interested in that? He stuck the file back in and shelved the mystery for the time being.

～

Since Pepper knew that Slim had no family, she made sure that she was there when they took him back for his catheterization. She had promised Gabe and Sam to report back to them. The chest x-rays were clear of any tumors and the lung function tests didn't show any signs of COPD or emphysema and they were now checking for any heart blockages.

"Slim I'll be here when they bring you out."

"I'm sure ya got better thangs to do then hover over me."

"Nope not really."

"I thank ya fer that."

The cardiac nurse came in to wheel Slim into the heart cath lab and Pepper said, "I'll see you when they finish with the test. It will be over before you know it."

"If something were ta happen ta me, take care of my little Gus."

"Nothing is going to happen, but I promise you that I will make sure Gus is well taken care of."

She felt oddly emotional watching him get wheeled away. He looked so scrawny in that hospital gown with his tufts of gray hair sticking out everywhere, and his weathered skin seemed so thin and fragile. His faded blue gray eyes had looked into hers for a moment and she swore she detected relief and gratitude that she was there. He was so alone. She wondered if he had ever had a family or a true love. Someday she hoped to hear his story.

About an hour had gone by and the doctor appeared and told Pepper that Slim had several blocked arteries that they were leaving alone, but the main artery to the back of the heart was over 90 percent blocked. They were going to try and open it with angioplasty then put a stent in. In the case they weren't successful, OR was on standby, prepared to do open heart surgery.

"Thanks for letting me know Dr. King. Take good care of my friend."

"He's a real character," Dr King said.

"That he is."

Keeping her promise to update Gabe, she dialed his number and left a message on his voice mail. An hour later she was surprised to look up and see Gabe and Annie enter the waiting room.

"Any more news?" Gabe asked.

"No, not yet. I consider that a good sign. If they were going to run into trouble they probably would have by now. I suspect they're having success with the angioplasty."

"I hope he doesn't have to go through open heart surgery," Annie said.

"I know," Pepper said.

"I brought a deck of cards, anybody in?" Gabe said.

"Start shuffling," Pepper said. "I hate waiting." The three sat down at the round table and Gabe dealt out a hand of cards to kill the time until they got news about Slim.

～

Several hours later, they all listened to the Doctors prognosis, "He is in recovery. The procedure was successful so now it's just a matter of him resting and healing. We'll keep him overnight for observation. He has suffered a slight heart attack at some point, but·no major damage. Hopefully he can kick the cigarette habit and barring complications, he should be back to normal in a week or two."

"Great news!" Gabe said.

"Thank God!" Pepper said. "Thank you, Dr. King."

"It's always a pleasure to be able to report good

news. Have a good day," he said, and briskly walked away.

They all looked at each other, their relief palpable. "Well I guess I'll get back to the salon; my afternoon and evening are jam-packed," Annie said.

"Go, I'll stick around until Slim is allowed to have visitors," Pepper said.

"I'm going to stay long enough to say hi, then I'll have to get back to the farm," Gabe said.

Annie gave Gabe a kiss on the cheek and left after getting assurances that they would keep her informed. She hated to leave but knew she wasn't needed and those most important to Slim would be there for him.

CHAPTER 25

"I think I'd like to go a little blonder this time," Annie's client requested.

"As is platinum?"

"Yes."

"I think we should pull a darker shade in as well to make it look more dimensional and natural," Annie said.

"Whatever you think. I trust you completely."

The door jingled and Annie looked up to see the same girl that had been in Gabe's arms at the bar, walk in. This couldn't be good. *Robbie.*

"I need to talk to you!" Robbie said in obvious distress.

"I'm sorry but it will have to wait. As you can see, I'm with a client."

"That might seem like a priority to you, but honestly I don't give a damn about your client or your business!"

Annie stepped away from her client and walked over to stand directly in front of Robbie saying firmly, "You might not give a damn, but I do. If you have something to say to me, we will do it in private. Excuse us Sue, this will only take a minute," Annie said to her client, as she steered Robbie to her back office.

Shutting the door Annie said, "Now what is this about?"

"Do you have any idea what you have done?" Robbie said.

"Um, that would be a no."

"Since Gabe won't man up, I guess it's up to me to fill you in. I'm pregnant. With Gabe's baby. We were trying to work on things before you entered the picture."

Annie's face lost all its color and her eyes grew wide in shock.

"I can see by your expression that he hasn't told you. Typical."

"I don't know what to say. Of course, I had no idea."

"Well I thought you should know. I'm sure you wouldn't want to ruin any chance we have, especially with an innocent baby on the way. One that deserves to have a father in the picture. I wanted to give you a chance to do the right thing," she said.

"I don't want to be insensitive, but I was under the impression that there never was any relationship between you two and that your one-night stand was a long time ago," Annie said.

"He would say that. I know that I was a convenient piece of ass when he needed it. But it was more than that to me. He used me, led me on and now doesn't want to take responsibility for the consequences of his actions. But don't believe him when he tries to say it was only a one-night stand."

"I'm not sure what you want me to say or for that matter to do. Isn't this between you and Gabe?"

"What do you think I want you to do? Take yourself out of the equation. He doesn't need the temptation of you pulling him away from doing what's right. He obviously isn't strong enough to do it on his own."

"I need to get back to my client now. Thank you for telling me and I wish you all the luck in the world."

"I need more than luck. I need you to let go of Gabe. He won't come back to me with you in the picture," Robbie said.

"And that is between Gabe and me. I need you to go now."

"I hope you'll do the unselfish thing and put yourself in my place. You are the one that will have to live with your decisions. I'll let myself out."

Annie sat down heavily at her desk. She needed a minute to pull herself together before returning to her client. *I can't do this!* But she would and she could. *Suck it up and put on your professional cap girl, you got this.*

Returning to her client Annie said, "Thanks for waiting, now about that color…"

"Are you alright? You look like you've seen a ghost," her client said.

"I'm fine I just received some unexpected news, but I'll be fine."

"If you're sure, Annie we can always reschedule, I'm okay with that."

"Thank you but no, don't worry. The distraction will be good for me."

"I won't pry but if you need to vent, I'm right here."

"Thanks Sue."

~

*A*nnie managed to hold it together until she finished with her last client for the day. She had worked alone for most of the day, but Zoey had showed up while Annie was working on her last cut and immediately sensed that Annie was not her usual cheerful self.

"Can I see you for a minute in the back room?" Zoey asked.

"I'm kind of in a hurry," Annie said, putting her friend off.

"It will only take a sec."

Annie followed her into the office and Zoey closed the door behind them.

"Spit it out. What's wrong?"

"I can't talk it about it right now or I'll fall apart."

"What did he do?" Zoey said.

Annie held her belly like she was about to be sick and said, "A girl came in and interrupted me with a client today to inform me that she is pregnant with Gabe's child."

"Oh my God! Is she legit?"

"I saw her with Gabe when I went to one of his shows. He told me that he had a fling with her, supposedly only once, a long time ago."

"I'm so sorry Annie."

"I've really got to go," she said, tears welling in her eyes.

"I'll check in with you later, but if you need me now, I can cancel my appointments and come with you."

"No. I'm supposed to have dinner at his place

tonight. I think I'm going to show up anyway and give him a piece of my mind!"

"Make sure you give him a chance to explain."

"What's to explain? My fear of getting involved with him was well-founded after all."

"Don't go assuming you know everything."

"He admitted to me that he had a fling with her, I'm sure the pregnancy wasn't planned, but he lied to me. He said it was over a long time ago. She isn't even showing much yet. I wouldn't put her over three to four months along at best."

"There are two sides to every story."

"This changes everything, I refuse to be that girl," Annie said, choking back tears. "She said they had been trying to work things out until I came along."

"Oh honey." Zoey wrapped her arms around her friend and rocked her while Annie cried quietly into her shoulder. "Promise me you'll keep your date tonight and let him explain."

"Zoey, after my disastrous relationship with Bradley ended, I had decided to take a long break from dating, then Gabe appeared and despite my best intentions I fell for him. I'm afraid that I'll always have terrible judgement when it comes to men!"

"Don't say that. You can't blame yourself for this and by the way, Gabe can be a great guy and still make mistakes. Nobody is perfect."

"I've really got to go...thanks Zoey, you know I appreciate you," Annie said.

"I know this is a huge blow, take care. Hopefully I'll see you tomorrow then?"

"Hopefully."

"Good luck!"

Giving her a watery smile, Annie hurriedly left the salon before she broke down for real. Safely in her car the dam broke and sobs racked her body. She cried so hard that she felt like she couldn't catch her breath. Her phone rang and she let it go straight to voicemail. With a heavy heart she headed toward the farm to confront Gabe.

CHAPTER 26

*G*abe couldn't wait to have Annie in his arms again. Opening the oven door, he checked on the enchiladas to see if the cheese was bubbling yet. The timer said there was still ten minutes to go. He frowned at his wristwatch. Annie was late. That was unusual for her.

He glanced around his tiny kitchen, satisfied that he had pulled it all together. Checkered tablecloth, tapered candles burning, wine glasses, wine chilling in the champagne bucket, a dozen red roses in the center vase, now all he needed was his date.

The back door opened and there she was. The first thing Gabe noticed was her bright red nose. "Annie girl, have you been crying?" He walked over to her and lifted her chin to look into her eyes. "Baby what's wrong?" He attempted to pull her into his arms, but she jerked away from him like she'd been burnt.

"How could you?" she blurted out.

He was so thrown he reeled like he'd been struck. "How could I what?"

"Why didn't you just level with me? I can always handle the truth, it's the lies I can't deal with."

"Whoa! What the hell are you talking about?"

"Robbie, remember her? Your baby mama."

"What the fuck are you talking about Annie? You aren't making any sense."

"Robbie paid me a little visit at my salon today," she said.

"And?" Gabe said, his temper rising as his voice became lower.

"I'd say about four months along or less. But you can probably tell me?"

"Let me guess, and she told you some fantastical tale about me being the father and you believed her?"

"You admitted it yourself, you had sex with her!"

"I shared with you that we had a one-night mistake many months ago, period."

"Well first of all, it must not have been that long ago, since she said you two were working on your relationship until I came along."

"And of course, knowing nothing about her, never having met her or had any kind of conversation with her your entire life, you immediately knew she was telling the gospel truth. Wow Annie, thanks for giving me the benefit of the doubt. You're the greatest."

"What am I supposed to think? I caught you two embracing in the back room at your show. She is beautiful…" her voice trailed off.

He slammed his fist down on the kitchen counter. "I'm blown away that after all we've shared you can believe that about me. You really think I'd lie about something as important as a child? You must really have a high opinion of me."

"Are you saying it's not true?"

"Believe what you want to believe Annie," Gabe said.

"She was very convincing. She said it was "typical" that you chose not to tell me about the baby and that I should step aside so that the child could grow up with a father."

"Are you done?" Gabe said in a steely tone.

"That's it? That's all you have to say for yourself?" Annie asked.

"You have it all figured out, what else is there for me to say?"

"Fine then! Have a nice life. I'm sure you, Robbie, and baby will be very happy together! Good thing you found that farmhouse. This place would have been much too small for the three of you," Annie said, choking back her sob as she turned and ran out the door, slamming it behind her as hard as she could.

As the door banged shut, the timer for the enchiladas went off. Gabe turned it off, removed the casserole from the oven and dumped the entire contents in the trash can. Then he took the roses from the table and went outside and threw them onto his compost pile.

He was beyond pissed. Furious with Robbie for her manipulation, but even more angry with Annie for believing a complete stranger over him. He had told Annie that Robbie wanted him back and that she thought she was in love with him. How hard was it for her to figure out from there that Robbie might try to sabotage their relationship? Underneath his anger was a deep hurt. Her level of distrust in men ran deep. He had thought that they had something special and had moved past her fears. *Wrong.*

Gabe put the wine in the fridge and pulled out a beer for himself. He decided to sit outside and have himself a little fire. Maybe the crickets and stars could sooth his soul tonight. The beer couldn't hurt either.

As Gabe's anger died down despair set in. He had to acknowledge to himself that the reason he was so angry and hurt, was that he had developed deep feelings for Annie. Who was he kidding, he had fallen in love with her. She was it for him. She was the one he wanted to wake up beside for the rest of his life. He felt like he was losing the best thing that had ever happened to him. He also knew that you couldn't make someone trust you, all you could do was be trustworthy, the leap of faith had to come from them.

As he was finishing his third beer, he thought he saw a shadow moving about by the barn. He put his bottle down and stealthily went to investigate. Keeping his back against the side of the barn wall, he made his way to the interior where the horse stalls were. Since it was summer the whole herd was turned out in the pastures all night.

He could see the shadowy figure down the long aisle in the very last stall. *Midnights stall.* He silently approached, so familiar with his surroundings, Gabe could have found his way blindfolded. The intruder must have sensed someone was there because suddenly they bolted out of the stall and quickly climbed the end gate and took off running.

Gabe knew with their head start, he'd never catch up, so he turned on the barn lights to see if he could figure out what they'd been up too. The horses' flakes of hay were already thrown into the stalls, ready for their morning feed.

Mixed in with the hay was something that made the hair stand up on Gabe's neck, it looked like a fern with a bunch of triangular-shaped leaves. Gabe thought it might be Bracken Fern which was highly toxic to horses and unfortunately tasted really good to them. Large amounts could kill a horse, but even in small amounts it contained toxins that could cause neurological damage. He decided to go wake up Sam and see how he wanted to handle this.

~

"Why only Midnight's stall?" Sam said. Bella sniffed around furiously where the intruder had been.

"Maybe they didn't have time to get to the rest," Gabe answered. Noticing Bella's agitation, he said, "Who's been here girl?"

She barked her response.

"We'll need to file a police report."

"Do you think I should call now or wait until the morning?"

"I think we can wait until morning," Sam said. "Maybe it's time to think about installing some security cameras for the barn and alarms for my clinic and the office."

"I'll get on that first thing in the morning after I file a police report," Gabe said.

~

*W*hen Annie left Gabe's, she went directly to Darcy's house. Her sister made her a cup of hot tea and settled in on the comfy living room couch for a long talk.

"Annie, you didn't even give the man a chance to tell you his side of the story. No wonder he's pissed."

"He didn't even try to fight for us... for me," She replied, wiping her eyes with her sleeve.

"You didn't ask, you accused. I am sure he felt hurt. I just don't believe Robbie's version. It doesn't add up to the person I know Gabe to be," Darcy said, firmly.

"I only know that when Robbie came into the salon, I was horrified by her revelation."

Darcy patted Annie's shoulder, "I can only imagine—you were totally unprepared, it must have been shocking."

"It was. It brought up all the old, well not quite so old, doubt again. You know my track record with men. It threw me into a tailspin. Maybe I still have terrible judgement when it comes to men, maybe I have been fooling myself and he's been using me. All the fears came rising up in me again."

"It's never too late to admit when you're wrong and apologize. When we know we've made a mistake that's what we do, we say we're sorry," Darcy said.

"I'm still not a hundred percent sure that it isn't true. Am I a terrible person for thinking that way?"

"No, you're just learning to trust yourself again. It's human to have doubts. You have been through a lot with Bradley and the guy before that. Don't beat yourself up. Sleep on it and see how you feel in the morning."

"Darcy, I am in love with him! This is terrible, I didn't want to be, it just happened." Her shoulders heaved as she sobbed.

Darcy got up to get some tissues and then took her little sister into her arms. "Annie you and Gabe are probably the last to know that you're both in love with each other. It's been obvious to the rest of us."

Annie smiled through her tears, "You think he is in love with me?"

"Duh."

"Even if it's true that it's his baby, we could get through that, I just can't handle lying."

"Like I said, sleep on it, the answers will come. Your bed is here is ready and waiting."

"Maybe I can convince one of the dogs to endure sleeping with me instead of you," Annie said.

"If not, bribing works wonders with these beggars."

"Good point," Annie said, already feeling calmer. Getting up from the couch she grabbed a dog biscuit from the bowl on the counter, "I guess I'll head to bed now I'm fried. Fannie, will you sacrifice yourself for the greater good?" Annie said holding the treat out temptingly.

Fannie barked her enthusiastic reply. "Let's go then, night sis," she said, and they both headed to the guest suite.

CHAPTER 27

"Any ideas of who might want to sabotage you or Parker Farms?" Police officer Connie Gibbons was doing the questioning, while her partner surveyed the scene and took photographs.

Gabe and Sam both shook their heads no.

"Any disgruntled ex-employees, or clients that lost a pet and think it's your fault Dr Parker?"

"Nothing comes to mind," Sam replied.

"Any jilted lovers that might have a vendetta against either of you?"

Gabe pinched the bridge of his nose looking down at the ground, "Not anyone that would do something like this," he said.

"You never know what a person is capable of, especially it there is jealousy involved," she said. "If someone comes to mind, best to tell us about it so we can either clear them or arrest them for vandalizing your property."

"I'm sure it wasn't her, for one thing I could tell it

was a dude, and apparently she is pregnant so I can't see her leaping over that fence and running like the person last night did," Gabe explained.

"She could have someone who would do her dirty work for her," Officer Gibbons replied. "You board horses here, you might want to check with each of the owners to find out if they have had any run-ins with anyone lately."

"We'll do that. We need to inform them about what happened anyway. They have a right to know. I have a security company coming out this afternoon to give us an estimate on installing cameras and alarms," Gabe said.

"Not a bad idea in this day and age, sad fact." She glanced at her partner who nodded, letting her know that he had all he needed.

"We'll file a report back at the station, in the meantime it's important that if you think of anything that you forgot to tell us or anything that comes to mind even if it seems insignificant, call me," she said handing them each a card.

"Thanks, officer," Gabe said.

"We appreciate your thoroughness," Sam said.

Getting behind the wheel of her police cruiser she said, "We'll be in touch."

"What's going on? I just saw the cops leaving," Cal said, making an appearance.

"Some vandalism. Gabe saw someone in the barn last night, they got spooked and ran off but not before depositing a poisonous pile of ferns in Midnights stall," Sam said.

"I don't have much hope of them catching the

asshole, so I think prevention is our best line of defense," Gabe said to Sam.

"I agree, but sometimes you get lucky."

"You know Sam, there is something that didn't occur to me until this very moment, recently someone tried to run me off the road when I was on my motorcycle."

"What? When did this happen?"

"Several weeks ago, while you were away. I honestly had forgotten about it, but at the time I was pretty shook up."

"Where were you riding?"

"It happened on the stretch of road right before the turn-off to the farm. Just as fast as the truck came up on my ass, it stopped and turned back around and sped away. I was assuming that it was some young punk wanting to fuck with someone, and it worked."

"Damn Gabe, that is some scary shit!" Cal said.

"I definitely think it's worth mentioning to the police." Sam said.

"I don't see how it's connected but I'll mention it next time I talk to them."

"I don't have a good feeling about all of this," Sam said.

"Nor do I."

"Stay alert. I'm going to the hospital to pick up Slim this morning, I'll fill him in."

"Cal you need to double and triple check everything from now on. Check the hay before bringing the horses in, double check the gates, check the grain, be hypervigilant!" Gabe said.

"Yessir."

"There is a cold wind blowing and I don't like it one bit. It is some kind of evil to try to harm an innocent animal," Gabe said. "Right now, since we're down a hand with Slim out, we'd better get moving. I have a lot to get done before the security folks arrive."

"Security?" Cal asked.

"Yeah, we're having cameras and alarms installed as soon as possible."

"Wow, this is serious then," Cal said.

"It doesn't get much more serious than this for a horse farm and vet clinic," Sam said. "Our boarders and patients are dependent on us one hundred percent; if that trust crumbles we are out of business. I'll be back in an hour or so, then I have half a day of barn calls to wade through and hopefully no emergencies coming in. See ya."

Gabe returned to the office to take care of a few things before starting the barn chores. He rubbed his hands over his face then through his hair. He was tired. *The only good to come out of this is I haven't had time to wallow in my own misery.*

It was going to be a long day because he had a gig tonight at the Dew Drop Inn. He was happy for the distraction since he had plenty of time to think about Annie when he was lying awake in bed tossing and turning.

CHAPTER 28

*A*nnie only had one more client to get through before she could leave. She was glad it was just a cut. James was still there, and she was happy for the company. She had filled him in on what had transpired between she and Gabe since he had missed the salon scene with Robbie. He was on the same page as Darcy, that Annie had jumped the gun and not given him a chance.

"I am relying heavily on you and Darcy's opinion, J.J.," Annie said. "I know Gabe has a gig tonight and I am going to show up and see if we can work something out."

"Good call."

"I hope so, my heart can't take another beating."

"You're stronger than you think. I'll bet he's as miserable as you are Annie."

"I hope so. I guess I'll find out tonight."

"What are you going to wear?" J.J. asked.

"Something incredibly sexy to remind him of what

he is missing."

"You could wear a bag and look sexy. You just have the IT factor."

"Thanks for the vote of confidence, I'm sure I'll need it round about nine o'clock tonight. Send me some positive vibes."

"I will darlin'."

.   ⌒

The parking lot was jam-packed when Annie pulled in and she had to park along the street. She could hear the music from outside the door as she approached. She tugged at her black knit mini skirt which was riding high up on her thighs. The silky cropped tank top didn't quite reach her waist, allowing fleeting glimpses of skin. The champagne colored Jimmy Choo knock-offs had stiletto heels and sparkled with glitter. She had swept up her hair in a twist leaving some wispy tendrils loose. Her eyeliner and dark brows made her green eyes pop. Annie was prepared for battle.

There were several people ahead of her showing their IDs to gain entrance. She pulled out her driver's license and handed it to the bouncer when it was her turn. He looked her up and down from head to toe and smiled approvingly. She smiled back and entered the fray.

She squeezed her way through the throng of people to get to the bar, which was three-deep with folks waiting to place their drink orders.

The opening band sang a Merle Haggard tune and didn't sound too bad. Annie glanced down the bar and caught sight of Gabe sitting on a bar stool. Her heart skipped a beat then started racing. *God he was so gorgeous.* He had a rare quality that was obvious but impossible to describe. *Star dust.*

She was so engrossed with Gabe that the bartender had to yell at her twice over the noise to get her order. "I'll have a vodka and tonic with a twist of lime," she said.

As she was planning her line of attack, a buxom blond sat down next to Gabe and leaned in to whisper something in his ear. Gabe laughed at whatever she had said causing Annie to shrink up inside. It was obvious that they were flirting with each other by their body language. Gabe threw back a shot and nodded to the bartender for another. The blond had wrapped her arm around Gabe's neck possessively and leaned in to kiss his cheek.

He was most definitely not resisting! Annie could feel her cheeks grow hot with humiliation. So much for reconciliation. He sure as hell wasn't wasting any time crying in his beer. *Fuck him!*

She quickly paid for her drink then got up to leave. Glancing back one last time, she was glad to note that Gabe had not noticed her. *Good and good riddance!*

~

*T*he blond hanging all over Gabe tonight was not a distraction. If anything, it only made him miss Annie more. He completely related to the saying "lonely in a crowd" because he embodied that sentiment. He was going through the motions, but his heart wasn't in it. The numbing effect of the whiskey wasn't nearly enough.

The blond, Courtney, was a beauty, but it all felt forced and fake. She was trying too hard and Gabe just wasn't interested. He was bored out of his mind with superficial small talk and meaningless hookups. It just didn't appeal to him anymore. He wanted one woman and that girl was Annie.

Too bad she had branded him a cheater and a liar. He couldn't seem to let go of the hurt and anger he felt. They had fit together like Johnny Cash and June Carter. Their chemistry was off the charts, but it was more than that. They spoke the same language. They never had to waste energy trying to explain what they were saying to each other or what they meant. They played well together and laughed a lot.

He had never been so stimulated and content at the same time. He felt like he was home when he was with her. How could she have believed a total stranger over him? Guilty until proven innocent. He just didn't get it.

Courtney returned from the restroom and rubbed her breasts against Gabe's back, as she nuzzled his neck from behind. "Hey, no offense Courtney, but I'm not available. We're getting ready to go on in a few minutes, so I hope you have a great night," Gabe said in his gentlest tone of voice.

Courtney reared back as if he had struck her and lashed out angrily, "You mean you have been leading me on all night and you're taken?"

"I haven't been leading you, on I've been sitting here getting drunk."

"You certainly didn't tell me to go away."

"I'm telling you now," Gabe replied quietly.

"No problem, I'm sure any other guy in this joint would be happy to have my attention."

"I'm sure you're right, it's just not me, I'm sorry," Gabe said.

"Your loss." With her head held high she walked over to a good-looking guy a few stools down and made her move which was eagerly accepted.

Gabe finished his beer and headed for the stage. The rest of the band were already up there. Rocker said, "I thought I saw Annie come in a little while ago."

"Naw, I would have seen her, I was at the bar the whole time."

"Not too many girls look like Annie, I'm pretty sure it was her."

The crowd had gathered in front of the stage, so Gabe introduced the band and they began their first set. He lost himself in the music. Tonight's set list was going to be heavy on the heartbreak. That usually pleased the crowd because everyone knew what misery felt like. They started with an old Hank Williams tune, *I'm so lonesome I could cry.*

Oh yeah, fun times.

*A*nnie pulled away fuming. *That didn't take long! Bastard!*

She was so thankful that he hadn't seen her. That would have been beyond embarrassing. Now she knew. This time she was done for real! Nothing serious for the next ten years. Time to live her life for herself. This love stuff was too painful. How could she have been so off in her judgement? Everything had seemed so right. It almost made her feel crazy. Could she really be that fucked up? Apparently so.

She decided to head over to Finnegan's and see if

there was someone there to play pool with. Why waste her outfit on an empty condo? She needed a drink and some company. Gabe wasn't the only one that could dazzle. A little male admiration was just what she needed. She touched up her siren red lipstick and started the car.

The bar was hopping. Annie made her entrance to cat calls and whistles. The bartender, a friend of Darcy's called out to her, "Where's your sister?"

"Probably shacked up with that cowboy," she said. "I need something strong, what do you suggest?"

"You want it to taste good or burn on the way down?" he said, laughing.

"Both."

"How about a lemon drop martini?"

"Sold."

She watched as he wet the rim of a glass and dipped it in sugar before putting ice in a shaker with the ingredients and mixing. He poured the concoction into the glass and passed it across the bar, "It's on me."

"Thanks, mmm, so good," she said, sipping the cocktail.

"Doesn't take too many of those to get a buzz going," he said.

"Good." Annie looked around the bar to see if she knew anyone and decided to put her quarters up on the table regardless. She might have a slight disadvantage with the mini skirt, but she was willing to try. Darts might be a better bet…*Oh well.*

A couple of guys were in the middle of a game when she placed her money down and they looked at each other and shook their heads. The dark-haired guy said, "The stakes just went up for sure."

"You got that right, suddenly I really want to kick your ass," he said, laughing as he took his turn, sinking the banked shot beautifully.

The dark-haired guy, whose name was Kip, won easily and he got the coveted chance to play against Annie. "You a regular here?" he asked.

"Not lately but I used to be," she replied. "Are you new in town?"

"Me and my buddy are just visiting. We're here on a business trip."

"What business is that?" Annie asked, curious because it was a small town and there weren't that many businesses around.

"We have an investment we are checking in on," he replied.

"Are you here for long?" Annie asked.

"Pretty much in and out," Kip answered.

"I'm intrigued."

Kip glanced at his buddy and they exchanged an inscrutable look, arousing Annie's interest further. "Let's talk about something more interesting, such as, how is it that a beauty like you happens to be tucked away in this tiny little town." Kip said.

Annie leaned over the table to take a shot, her tight skirt showing off her curvy behind and legs that went on for miles, "I was born and raised here. I own a salon in town, The Diamond."

"Too bad, I was going to offer to whisk you away with me," Kip said flirting outrageously, which was just what Annie had been hoping for when she decided to hit the bar.

"Whisk me away to where?"

"Kentucky, can't you tell by my accent?"

"I didn't want to assume," she said, laughing, "but yeah you have a pretty definite southern drawl."

"Good shot," Kip said. Annie smiled and put two more balls in before missing her third.

"Are either of you ready for another drink?" Kips friend asked.

"Yeah, put it on my tab Roy, I'll take a shot of Kentucky bourbon along with my beer."

"I'll have another. The bartender knows what I'm drinking," Annie said.

Kip walked over to Annie and put his arm around her waist. his hand resting on her hip. He was quite handsome and although flattered by the attention, and her bruised ego craving validation, she just wasn't into him. She realized that maybe this hadn't been the best idea after all. She only wanted Gabe. *Empty.*

Annie side stepped out of his arm and chalked up her cue stick before taking her last shot and sinking the eight ball. "Beat ya!"

Not to be brushed aside Kip put his arm around her again, "Annie you are about as hot as it gets. What do ya say we go back to my hotel and get to know each other a little better?" Annie tried wiggling out from his grip, but he was stronger and slightly drunk, so he didn't pick up on her hints.

"Sorry Kip but I'm not into one-night stands," she replied firmly, taking ahold of his arm and peeling it off her body.

Not accustomed to being rejected he persisted, "Nobody has to know but me and you. We could have some fun. I know all the ways to please a lady."

"I'm sure that you do but the answer is still no."

Roy returned with their drinks and Annie decided it

was a good time to extricate herself. "Thanks for the game and the drink, safe travels to you both."

"You have no idea what you're missing. Have you heard of Worthington Farms?" Kip asked, his arrogance showing.

"No, I can't say that I have."

"Look it up, I'm a partner. I could fly you anywhere in the world you want to go. Wine, dine, play, whatever your heart desires. I accept that you're not into one-night stands but how about becoming my mistress?"

"Great so you're married? You don't take no for an answer, do you?"

"Not when it comes to someone as stunning as you, you literally take my breath away. I am enchanted," he said.

"You are also full of yourself, goodbye."

Annie turned and almost ran into Bradley who had come up behind her.

"Bradley!"

"Annie, are these guys bothering you?"

"No, I'm fine."

"Oh God, it is so good to see you!" Bradley said.

Jesus can't a girl just go out and have a couple of drinks? "I'm just leaving, have a good night."

"Wait, I'll walk you to your car."

"No thank you, I am capable of seeing myself out."

Bradley's expression darkened but he quickly veiled it, "Been sleeping at loverboy's farm lately?"

"And that is your business… because?"

"You *are* my business, Annie."

"Men!" Annie said in disgust as she strode out of the bar alone.

CHAPTER 29

*S*am walked into the office and sat across from Gabe who was catching up with paperwork. "Thanks for taking care of the security system, I probably should have done that a long time ago."

"No problem," Gabe replied.

"Darcy told me about you and Annie, do you want to talk about it?"

"Not really," he said.

"I guess I shouldn't have asked because I have something I'd like to say, whether you want to hear it or not," Sam said.

"Shoot then," Gabe replied.

"Look I know these Morgan girls are stubborn, but you have to see it from Annie's side as well. I know you well enough to say with conviction that Robbie was lying, but I've got no skin in the game."

"She should trust me by now and she could at least have had the decency to hear me out!"

"I know all that but Gabe, she is in love and that makes her vulnerable. She has a high EQ."

"EQ? What the hell is that?" Gabe asked.

"It's like IQ but it's emotional intelligence. It's what makes her so special. She thinks through her heart. That is why she will never be boring, or mean spirited, why she is so fun to be with. She has the smarts and the feelings."

"I'm still pissed off. I don't need the drama. If she can't handle the heat, I don't know what I can do about it."

"Are you sure about that? Don't you think you're being a bit of a butthead?"

"Sam how do you think I feel? I was blindsided. I had no idea Robbie was pregnant! It's been well over nine months since I had sex with her."

"Did you tell Annie that?"

"She didn't give me a chance to."

"You don't need her permission; you make sure she hears it. Frankly I'm surprised that you didn't fight a little harder Gabe," Sam said.

Gabe didn't like the feeling of knowing he had disappointed his hero. He respected Sam and knew if Sam was saying it, he had to listen.

"I guess you think I'm in the wrong here?"

"I'm not saying it's all on you, but you certainly played a part."

"Do you think she'll listen to me now?"

"What have you got to lose? We all need reassurance from time to time, no matter how old we are, and our emotional baggage comes along with us. It dissipates, but sometimes it can rear its head at the most unexpected times. Don't be too hard on yourself or Annie," Sam said.

"I'll think about what you've said," Gabe said.

"That's good enough for me. In my opinion, it's just a bump in the road for you two. You will either become stronger together because of this or you'll decide it's not a good match. I'm betting on the former."

"Thanks Sam."

"You know I love you like a brother," Sam said as he got up to leave.

"Yeah I know, now let me get back to work."

Gabe just sat there for a while pondering Sam's words. From anyone else Gabe would have told them to go fuck themselves, but from Sam it was different. He trusted him completely and knew Sam would never steer him wrong.

He picked up the phone and dialed the local florist and ordered a dozen roses a mix of red and white, to be delivered to the salon. Now that he had made the shift from anger to humility, he was desperate to have it out with Annie. He needed her. He now wondered what had took him so long. He hadn't seen her for over a week and he was hurting. He hoped she felt the same.

~

*A*nnie was shampooing her first customer when she saw the huge vase of deep red roses delivered. J.J. took the flowers from the driver and peaked at the card. "Annie, these are for you."

Annie's face lost all its color. "Are you sure?"

"Yep, plain as the nose on your face, the envelope

says Annie Morgan. Red roses, true love," he said. "It's about fricking time."

The customer getting her hair rinsed said, "Go ahead and read the card."

"I'll wait."

"No! The suspense is killing me," James said.

"You are a pain, do you know that?" she said, grumbling.

James took the tiny envelope over to Annie to open. Hand shaky, she slid her finger under the seal and pulled out the card.

I'm an idiot. I should have fought harder. Please forgive me! Gabe

"What does it say?" J.J. asked.

Annie read the card aloud and James clapped his hands with glee and said, "Finally, he admits it!"

Annie's eyes were decidedly moist as she wrapped her customers hair in a towel. "Let's move over to my station," she said.

"Those roses are gorgeous," her client said.

"Yes, they are the most beautiful flowers I have ever seen," Annie said.

~

"Gabe, it's Annie. God it's so good to hear your voice."

"Thanks for the flowers," she said.

"Babe, it's not nearly enough. I'm sorry, I was a fool. I should have been more understanding. When can I see you? I need to explain."

"Tonight?"

"Yes! I was hoping you'd say that. Dinner out?"

"Yes," Annie agreed. "I can come over to the farm and we can leave from there," she offered.

"I'll make reservations for seven thirty if that works for you?"

"Perfect."

"Annie, I'm sorry."

Silence.

"Are you still there?" Gabe asked.

"Yes, I'm here. See you tonight."

❧

The salon was hopping, with all but one of the stylists working. Annie volunteered to go pick up their lunch order which had been phoned in to the diner. As she walked in, she saw Cal seated at the counter, next to none other than Kip and Roy, from the other night. They were deep in conversation when Annie startled Cal by greeting him.

"Hi Cal." Looking curiously at his companions she said, "Do you know these guys?"

"Naw, I just recognized the accent, fellow Kentuckians."

Kip had the good sense to look a little sheepish as he greeted Annie, "Hi Annie. Sorry if I came on too strong the other night. A little too much to drink."

"Yeah, well, wasn't my favorite part of the evening. I thought you were going to be "In and out"?" she said.

"We had to stay on an extra couple of days."

The waitress brought her the bags containing the carryout containers and Annie paid at the register. "Well happy trails," she said.

"I'm just leaving, do you need help carrying those to your car?" Cal asked.

"No thanks Cal, I appreciate the offer though," Annie said, smiling warmly at him.

"I'll walk out with you," he said. "Hey, I'm real sorry about you and Gabe. I hadn't seen you around, so I asked about it and found out you two had broken up."

Annie shrugged her shoulders, "We took a break, we're getting together tonight, we'll see what happens."

"Good. You two seem perfect for each other."

"I gave up on perfection a long time ago," Annie smiled affectionately at Cal, "But that doesn't mean you have to. I'll hopefully see you around."

"Bye Annie."

"Bye Cal, don't work too hard."

"Never," he said. Grinning, "But don't tell my boss that."

Annie mimicked zipping her lip shut and got in her car and drove away.

CHAPTER 30

*G*abe was pacing the floors then suddenly there she was. His breath caught and his throat closed. Her hair was cascaded in thick red waves around her bare shoulders. She wore a black silky pantsuit, cinched at the waist with the front open in a vee all the way to the belt line, showing off her flawless honey-toned skin. The pants were loose fitting with the rest of the garment hugging her torso like a glove.

He approached her slowly, unsure of himself, "Annie," was all he could croak out.

"Gabe, you look great," Annie said, and he did. Black jeans, tucked-in white dress shirt, same wild mop of hair, dreamy eyes, she felt tongue tied.

They both started to speak at the same time, then laughed with Gabe saying, "Let me go first. Annie, I am so sorry, I really fucked up. I was so angry I couldn't see it from your point of view and for that I apologize. I am a stubborn asshole and it could have cost me the most important thing in my life."

"I'm sorry too. I was so shocked I just freaked out. I am ready to listen now. I should have given you a chance and I didn't."

He took another step toward her and she met him halfway. They embraced and Gabe buried his face in her hair, to breathe in the intoxicating scent of her. With a ragged breath he said, "I've missed you." And he covered her lips with his own and kissed her.

Gabe's fingers sank into her hair as he held her tight. She put her arms around his neck, opening her mouth wide to receive him. "Oh baby, you feel so good."

"Gabe," she responded breathlessly.

He slipped his hand under the silky material and cupped her breast, hearing her sharp intake of breath he smiled against her lips. "I'm glad I still have that effect on you."

"Always," she said.

"As much as I hate to say it, we better get going," Gabe said.

Her eyes were shimmering with desire. The heat between them almost unbearable. "If we don't leave now, we probably won't get there," she agreed.

He held her hand, intertwining their fingers, as he raised the back of her hand to his lips. "Thank you for giving me another chance."

"Thanks for the flowers," she said quietly.

"Anything to win my girl back. A rose for a rose," he said, grinning.

"You have a way with words cowboy."

*A*nnie felt her heart racing and the adrenaline surging through her body. Looking across the table into his eyes she was lost. His thick dark lashes surrounding those gorgeous greenish brown eyes, that seemed to change colors every time she was with him, and were currently almost gold, and were penetrating her soul. He was seducing her without uttering a word. He had been staring at her lips for the past several minutes and judging by the wetness between her thighs it was working.

"Annie, I haven't had sex with Robbie for well over nine months. I didn't have any idea that she was pregnant and I sure as hell am not the father. I am one hunderd percent willing to take a paternity test to prove it to you."

"I believe you. You don't need to take it for my sake, only if you need to prove it against Robbie's claim. But there is something I have to ask," she said.

"Ask away."

"Who was the blond you were with at your last gig?"

"So, you were there," Gabe said quietly. "Rocker said that he thought he saw you, but I didn't believe him."

"I was there. I had done a lot of thinking and felt I'd been unfair to you, so I showed up to talk about it. Then I saw you with another woman and it destroyed me," she admitted.

"Annie, I'm sure it didn't look good, but despite how it looked, I wasn't into her at all. It only made me feel lonelier and miss you more. It was empty. I blew her off before our first set. I'm sorry you had to see that. What a waste of a week. We could have been together all this time."

"Well I tried to have an evening of revenge flirtation, but it backfired. I ended up getting propositioned to be someone's mistress and ran into my ex. Altogether a pretty awful night." Their food arrived and suddenly Annie was famished. She hadn't had an appetite since the split but now she could hardly wait to dig in.

Gabe watched her devour her food with amusement. She looked like a good strong wind could carry her away, but boy could she eat. He liked her zest for life. He realized all the many ways that she was different from every other woman he had ever dated and was grateful that he had dodged a bullet. He had Sam to thank for that. He would be sure to tell him so at the first opportunity.

∼

They could hardly wait to get in the house before tearing each other's clothes off. The door barely shut behind them, before they tugged and pulled at each other's garments while kissing passionately. Annie unbuckled Gabe's belt and desperately pulled at his zipper. She could feel his hard length and reached inside his underwear to grip him firmly.

He moaned into her neck as he bit her ear lobe and pulled her straps down to expose her breasts. He picked Annie up and carried her into the bedroom to lay her down on his twin bed, then stepped out of his jeans and underwear. He stood there, gazing down at Annie, his full erection begging for release. Her eyes were glazed over with passion and she had no idea how provocative he found her. He slowly undressed her, pulling her pantsuit down her hips and thighs, finally leaving her exposed with only a dainty pair of lace panties and bra between them.

She watched him with lowered lids as his eyes bore holes into her skin. She felt scorched everywhere his gaze lingered. Annie had never felt so desired or beautiful. His raw animal desire for her matched her own for him. She needed to feel him inside of her. "Gabe, I need you now!" she said.

Annie watched him slowly and seductively remove her undergarments. He parted her thighs, nudging her knees apart. She studied his strong chest, his broad shoulders, the ripped abs, the lust written in his expression, the throbbing erection, and she thrust her pelvis in the air in agony for deliverance. He touched her labia with his thumb pressing then caressing until her body was wet and ready. Slipping on a condom, he plunged into her as she met him thrust for thrust.

He rode her hard, panting heavily, and reached a climax just as she did. They both cried out as their passion erupted. Gabe collapsed on top of Annie and nuzzled her wildly disarrayed hair then moved down to lick her nipples. "God, please tell me this isn't a dream," he said against her breasts. He began to gently suckle her.

She brushed his hair back from his forehead, cradling his head against her breast while he continued to skillfully arouse her again. She kissed the top of his head and with her nipple in his mouth he looked up at her through eyes filled with yearning. Watching him suckling aroused her all over again. Her vagina throbbed as he slipped his finger into her wetness. He rubbed her clitoris, pressing and stroking her with mastery, knowing all the right ways and places. He brought her to another orgasm while she writhed beneath him.

"My God! Your body," he said.

She rolled him onto his back rubbing her hands over his chest. She rubbed his shaft at the pubic bone then wrapped her palm around it and pulled. Teasing his tip with her thumb, she positioned herself over his penis, grabbed another condom, straddled his erection and slowly sank down...taking him inside of her all the way. She felt his entire penis fill her, his tip pressing deep inside. She began riding him up and down, leaning down for a kiss, her breasts brushed against his soft chest hair. He came hard and fast, crying out her name.

They were too spent to do anything but lay there. Soon after, they both dozed off, tangled up in each other's arms.

CHAPTER 31

"$\mathcal{I}$ saw a bright red Miata in the drive this morning," Sam said grinning.

"Yeah, and I have you to thank for that."

"I'm glad to be able to play cupid every now and then," he said.

"I'm serious, a thank you seems kind of lame, but I'm really indebted to you," Gabe said.

"You would have figured it out eventually. I may have saved you a little time is all," Sam said.

"Luckily we'll never have to find out whether or not I would have pulled my head out of my ass on my own," he said chuckling.

Sam studied the camera footage from the night before and said. "Gabe, come here and take a look at this."

"Holy shit! That's the cop that stopped by here that day a while back for a wellness check."

"Are you sure about that?" Sam asked.

"Yeah I'm sure."

"That happens to be Annie's ex," Sam said.

"You're shitting me, right?"

"Nope that's him. Now the question is, what in the hell was he doing prowling around here at midnight last night?"

"Damn, following Annie?"

"That'd be my guess."

"I'm going to call Darcy and get her over here to see this," Sam said.

"I knew he was trouble, but I guess I didn't realize how obsessed he was. She had a run in with him a few weeks ago and was pretty shaken up. Maybe I should have taken the situation more seriously."

"It's a hard call. A thin line between heartbreak and obsession." Sam said.

"I guess so," Gabe said, brows furrowed with worry.

"I haven't asked lately, how's Midnight progressing?"

"She is coming along. I'll hate to see her go. She is a special horse and I've grown quite attached."

"I'm sure that's the hard part."

"Not with all of them, but every once in a while, you get to work with one that feels soulful," Gabe said. "This is one of those rare connections."

"A great opportunity, and you deserve it."

"Thanks chief." Gabe saluted Sam as he left.

≈

"Oh my God, what in the world was he doing there?" Annie said, her eyes wide with fear.

"I hate seeing you afraid. I'm not going to let anything happen to you," Gabe said hugging her tightly to his chest.

"He must be losing it for real." Annie said.

"For now, it's best if you move in with me until everything resolves. We've got a virtual compound there with Sam, Slim, and me, plus the dogs."

"But that didn't stop him last night."

"We weren't wise to him then. Now we are," Gabe said, brushing her hair back as he kissed her forehead.

"I'm frightened Gabe."

"I know you are, and you need to be on your guard, but we're all here for you, the cops are going to investigate his trespassing, that might just be enough to spook him." She still looked doubtful.

"I'll kill the bastard if he tries to fuck with you again. He will have to get through me to get to you." Her fear broke Gabe's heart. "You trust me don't ya?" he asked gently.

She nodded yes. He tilted her head back and touched his lips to hers. Her breath shuddered then she began to kiss him back. Her desire broke through her fear for a moment as her body responded to him. She held him tight, wanting to forget everything but being held in his arms.

～

"The guy is unraveling!" Darcy said, a mixture of exasperation and anger in her voice. "There is no refuting the video evidence. It was Bradley."

"What do you think I should do about it?" Sam asked.

"You have to report it."

"Yes, but what about Annie? What if it makes him go completely unhinged?"

"I know but he's had countless warnings. What else can we do?" Darcy said.

"My concern is that he'll become more dangerous," Sam said.

"That's why we've held off until now, but I'm afraid he's left us no choice."

"He is desperate to have her back, not to harm her. I think it makes him crazy that she is with another guy."

As always, his demeanor calmed Darcy's nerves immediately. "I'm sure you're right. I have no love for the guy, but I don't think he is capable of actually harming her."

"We'll make sure Annie stays safe. Gabe wants her to sleep at his place for now. At work there are people around. She'll just have to be on the alert until things blow over."

"You're right, me scaring the shit out of myself won't help the situation any." Darcy conceded.

"Do you want to talk to the Captain before I report this?"

"Yes, I'll go over to the precinct now, actually, why don't you come with me?"

"Sure, let me tell Gabe what's happening then we can take off."

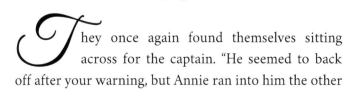

They once again found themselves sitting across for the captain. "He seemed to back off after your warning, but Annie ran into him the other night and I'm thinking it stimulated his obsession," Darcy said.

Bob swiveled his chair drumming his desk with his fingers, "I see."

"I had some vandalism at my farm last week, so I had security cameras installed this past weekend. When I was reviewing last night's footage, this morning, Bradley could be seen on the premises around midnight. Annie happened to be spending the night there with my manager Gabe Hunter, who lives in the tenant farmhouse."

"Anything vandalized last night?"

"No. But when I played the tape for Gabe this morning, he informed me that it was the same guy that had showed up on duty in his police uniform a while back. The officer claimed he was responding to a call for a wellness check but when questioned he back pedaled and wouldn't provide any proof. When Gabe pushed back and tried to get his name and badge number he split."

"Annie is coming in this afternoon on her break to file a restraining order," Darcy added.

"His little stunt at the farm, if it indeed was a fake wellness check, was harassment plain and simple, but it's your word against his. However, the trespassing is criminal police misconduct and there is proof. I will file an incident report immediately. That will be placed in his file and there will be an internal investigation. He'll be placed on a desk job while the investigation is pending."

He looked deep in thought then said, "Safety is the most important factor here. Stalking is very hard to prove; a protection order is more enforceable.

Regardless, they'd wait to see how the case went before they would rule on a suspension or termination."

"That could take forever. I've been concerned about poking the beehive, as I mentioned last time," Darcy said. "Maybe she should hold off on filing for now."

"It's very complex, I know," Captain Gregory said.

"Thank you for your help Bob, we really appreciate your honesty," Darcy said.

"It really sucks that Annie is so vulnerable," Sam said.

"Make sure she isn't alone and that she carries pepper spray at all times."

"We'll do that. Keep me posted Captain," Darcy requested.

"I will. I'm sorry I couldn't be more helpful."

"At least we have the evidence."

"Yes, that's very important. Have a good day," The captain said.

"Thanks."

Darcy and Sam left the office discouraged and very concerned for Annie's safety. "Things always seemed stacked for the bad guys. It sucks," Darcy fumed. "Let's head over to the salon and fill Annie in."

Sam pulled out of the parking lot. "You read my mind."

CHAPTER 32

After work Annie and Gabe went to her condo to pack up some things and returned to Gabe's house to unload. Gabe had cleared a couple of drawers for her and designated half his bedroom closet to Annie. If it weren't for the circumstances she would be thrilled.

They went together like peanut butter and jelly. It just worked. She had never been in a relationship that was so easy. The sexual tension exhilarated her but they could also relax together, like they were currently doing. Sitting on the couch with her feet in his lap, the lights turned low, watching a movie while trying to forget about the danger lurking beyond these farmhouse walls.

She glanced over at Gabe. He had fallen asleep. He looked so handsome, feet propped up on the old coffee table, his head tipped back against the couch cushions, ink black lashes fanning his cheeks. It was all she could do to not wake him. Just looking at him aroused her.

But his workdays started at the crack of dawn, so she let him sleep on.

How will this all end? She let her thoughts drift and Robbie popped in, which led to her fantasizing about having Gabe's baby and wondering what he or she would look like. If it ever happened, she hoped they would have his eyes and hair. She hoped they would grow up to be kind like he was.

They would ride horses as soon as they could sit on one. They would grow up with dogs and chickens. They would never doubt that they were loved. She and Gabe shared that. They knew what it felt like to be rejected by a parent and that pattern would stop with them.

With as little disturbance as possible she switched ends and nestled her head into his lap. Still asleep, he automatically cupped his hand between her neck and shoulder, his fingertips resting on her collar bone. Annie couldn't stop herself from touching him and rested her hand on his thigh, her fingers inching up toward his groin. *Down girl, let him sleep!* She forced herself to pay attention to the movie and shortly after, she too, was sound asleep.

⁓

*A*nnie had decided to take a mental health day and canceled all her clients. It would be a major pain in the ass to get them back in, but she desperately needed the time off. Gabe had put her to work filling water buckets and giving the horses their morning grain and when they were turned back out, she helped muck the stalls. Slim came by to supervise and it seemed to Annie like he might be softening toward her.

"I reckin keepin busy is always good for chasin the devil away," he said.

"It does seem like a good distraction," Annie agreed.

"I'm here iffin ya need anything, I'm keepin my eye on things."

"Why thank you Slim," she said, touched by his words.

"Hain't nothin I wouldn't do fer anybody," he said.

Annie grinned. "I'm sure that's true Slim, I'm just glad to have you on my side for a change."

"I reckin Gabe's as close to a son as I got, I'd do prit near anything fer him, that includes cepting you."

"I'm not so bad once you get to know me," Annie said, laughing.

"I whittled ya something," he said.

"You did?" Annie practically squealed in delight.

He reached in his pocket and pulled out a small wooden four-leaf clover and handed it to her. "It's a clover," he said.

"I see that—it's lovely Slim, thank you."

"Count of ya being Irish and all, and bringin ya luck, I kin paint it green iffin ya want."

"No, I like it just as it is." Annie slipped it into the front pocket of her jeans and impulsively hugged Slim. He stiffened up but didn't pull away and that was a pretty good start as far as Annie was concerned. "I'm going to go find Gabe. He promised me that I could get on Midnight today."

"Best iffin ya keep that good luck charm close then," he said, grinning as he walked away.

Gabe was lunging Midnight when Annie found him

in the indoor arena. It was a striking image. The powerfully built black horse, shining like obsidian and the strong virile cowboy in his element taming the beast. Gabe's muscles bulged as he held the lunge line. He was shirtless, his back muscles defined and powerful. His jeans hugged low on his hips, his tan line showing slightly as he moved around.

Midnight noticed her before Gabe did, her ears suddenly pricking forward as she warily eyed Annie. Gabe brought her to a halt and motioned for Annie to approach.

"Here, why don't you lunge her first, let her get to know you a little better. You've lunged a horse before haven't ya?"

"Yes, I'll give it a try," Annie said taking the lunge line and rope from Gabe.

Clicking her tongue, she formed a triangle with Midnight, the line, and the crop urging her forward. Midnight immediately responded. She lunged in both directions then brought her to a walk.

"Good job, she trusts you," Gabe said.

"I am in love with her already… actually, it was love at first sight," Annie said.

"I know the feeling." Gabe winked at her and she flushed at the compliment.

"I think it'd be best if I lead you around the ring after you mount, let her get used to you. I'm the only one who has ridden her."

"Sounds good. I don't want to rush her. I also don't want to be tossed off if I can help it."

By the end of the ride, Annie was trotting around on her own, Midnight completely relaxed under saddle.

Annie cheeks flushed with excitement. She couldn't keep the elation from her voice as she dismounted.

"She trusts me!"

"Yes, she does, you did great!"

"Gabe all of your work has paid off, she is a dream to ride."

"That she is." He suddenly looked glum.

"I guess success in this case means letting go; it must be hard," Annie said.

"This one is gonna hurt," he agreed.

She put her arms around him and said, "You'll still have me to ride."

He laughed out loud. "There is that. Let's brush her and turn her out, then grab a bite to eat, how's that sound?"

"Like you read my mind."

CHAPTER 33

A week turned into two and they began to establish a routine. For Annie, it seemed like a yearning she had felt for as long as she could remember was finally being satisfied. There had been no further vandalism or trespassing, so everyone began to relax. She and Gabe were thriving together. That was the best way she could describe it.

Something mystical and inexplicable was happening to them. Some might call it kismet or fate, destiny or fortune, whatever it was Annie knew how lucky they were to have found each other. She was slowly trusting it all. When the doubts crept in, she pushed them aside. Gabe had not given her any reason to doubt that he felt the same way.

*A*s Gabe brushed Midnight, he was also mentally preparing to let go of her. She had blossomed under his tutelage. Her personality was beginning to shine as her confidence grew. His shoulders slumped as he thought about another transition and adjustment to go through. He only hoped that he had given her a strong enough foundation. She had proven to be resilient and courageous. Those were innate qualities he had nothing to do with, he had only helped her to find them in herself.

The trailer was scheduled to arrive the following Monday to pick her up, so he had six more days to work with her. He would make them count. Cal appeared and asked if there was anything else for him to do before leaving for the day.

"Did you throw some extra bales down from the loft? We're getting low."

"I forgot, I'll do that now," Cal said.

"That's it for today then, thanks for all your hard work."

"No problem. You're going to miss that filly aren't ya?"

"Yeah, unfortunately it goes with the territory," Gabe said.

"I suppose it does. I've never had that kind of connection with a horse, I guess it's 'cause I've never had the opportunity."

"I hope you get to experience it one day. There is almost nothing as deeply satisfying, only a few things I can think of," Gabe said, smiling.

"Does one of those happen to have red hair?"

"Um you could be on to something there."

"I'll catch ya later then," Cal said.

"See ya."

He was turning Midnight out when a black sedan pulled up. Curious, he walked toward the vehicle just as a stunning brunette got out. "Hey Gabe, long time no see."

"Brianna! What brings you to these parts?" he asked.

"Honestly? You," she said.

"Me? Last I knew you left me in a trail of dust and moved to California for your big break," Gabe said.

"Well, you know how that goes, it was pretty empty without you there."

"It's been two years since you dumped me, hard to believe it took you that long to decide you can't live without me," Gabe said, unable to keep the irony from his voice.

"That's just how special you are," she said seductively while reaching for his hand. "I've missed you Gabe. Hollywood men are narcissistic and shallow. You're the real deal."

"You're a bit too late, I'm afraid," he said kindly, just as Annie pulled up.

Gabe pulled away from Brianna's grasp but not before Annie caught them holding hands. She jumped out of the car like a sizzling firecracker.

"Really?" Annie said eyes blazing.

Brianna smiled condescendingly at Annie, while looking at Gabe from under her lashes. "Hi, I'm Brianna." She held out her hand toward Annie who chose to ignore it. "Gabe and I are old, um, I guess you'd say friends," she chuckled. "I just moved back to town and thought I'd look him up," she said.

"Oh? So, I'm interrupting a reunion, so sorry!" she said turning on her heel to leave.

"Annie, oh no you don't," Gabe said catching up with her and blocking her exit. "We're not going through this again."

"Move," she said between clenched teeth.

"Nope."

"I mean it Gabe! I have to get back to work. I was just stopping by on my break," she said.

"I'm sure you don't need to rush right off now do ya?" he said, impatience in his voice.

"As a matter of fact, I do," she retorted.

"Gabe, darling, let her go, that would give us a chance to catch up," she said, intentionally stirring the pot.

"If you don't get out of my way, I'm going to scream for Sam and have him make you," she said.

"Jesus Annie. Are you serious right now?"

"Yes, we can talk about this tonight when I get off work. I'll finish up around seven. That is if you're not busy," she said, her tone dripping with sarcasm.

"Seven then," he said, exasperated. "I'll have dinner ready."

He moved aside so she could get into her car and leave. He wasn't happy about it, but he knew she wasn't about to budge, and he was smart enough to admit defeat. Her stubbornness was on full display.

～

*A*nnie drove away fuming. It seemed like every time she turned around there was another beautiful woman throwing herself at Gabe. Dammit!

She didn't like this one bit. It kept knocking her off balance. Just when she let her guard down, someone else came along to burst her bubble.

In some ways she felt bad for Gabe. He couldn't help that he was so damn hot. But on the other hand she felt like throttling him. Her green-eyed monster was alive and well. It was a good thing she had work to distract her. Hopefully she would be able to contain her jealousy by dinner time.

$\sim$

Gabe had dinner ready for Annie when she arrived home from work.

"I'll set the table," Annie said coolly. "I'm going to miss this."

Gabe froze. "Miss this? Why, where are you going?"

"We knew it wasn't going to last forever Gabe. Now that things have calmed down, I thought I'd return to my condo. I've got bills to pay and cleaning to do, you know basic upkeep."

"I don't like it. I think it's a bad idea for all kinds of reasons," Gabe persisted.

"Gabe, I have to catch up on some things. It's like I've been on vacation and now reality is seeping back in."

"What about Bradley?"

"Since he got assigned to a desk job while they're doing an internal investigation, he won't do anything to jeopardize his chances. He has had two weeks to do something and hasn't."

"I don't feel nearly as confident as you seem to," Gabe said.

"Look according to Darcy, his argument to keep his

job is that he was worried about me since he couldn't reach me at home or by phone. He wanted to check up on me. Even though we know he's lying, he won't want to show them his hand. It's his word against mine now."

"Did the captain say anything else?"

"Not that I'm aware of."

"And of course, this has absolutely nothing to do with Brianna, right?" he said.

"I didn't say that. Look Gabe, I've gotten too comfortable. What are we doing? You and me. Playing house, one day slipping into the next, we haven't made any commitments. For all I know, Brianna was the love that got away. She is stunning. I just need some time alone. I'm in too deep. It scares me."

"I want it on record that I am opposed to this idea."

"Noted," Annie said.

"I'm not going to lie to you Annie, I was heartbroken when Brianna up and left me for the bright lights of California, but that was two years ago. I hadn't heard from her since, until today. I'm over her. When are you going to learn to trust me? Or more importantly, yourself?' he said quietly.

Annie impatiently swiped at a tear and said, "I don't know. Maybe never. Every time I get too comfortable something knocks me off balance. I told you from the beginning that I wasn't sure that I was up for competing for your affection."

"There is no competition Annie, I don't know how else to say it," He threw up his hands and turned away from her.

"Just forget it Gabe. I need time, and you won't convince me otherwise. Let's eat."

"Whatever you say, you're in charge. Sit down and dig in before supper gets cold," Gabe said.

They were both quiet as they ate dinner.

"You know Midnight is being shipped out next week," he said, attempting to make conversation.

"I know, I'm sorry Gabe, I know how much she means to you."

"What about how much you mean to me?"

Annie didn't respond. They finished the rest of the meal locked into their own stubbornness.

"Will you at least stay here tonight? I know you're upset, but we can just sleep together. That's all," Gabe said.

"It's late and I'm tired so that's a yes."

Gabe couldn't believe the relief he felt at her agreeing to stay. She hadn't given up completely. "I'll clear the table. Let's watch a movie, sound good to you?"

"Sure," she said, still subdued.

"I'll even let you pick."

"How about *The Other Woman?*" Annie said, smiling slightly at her own dark humor.

"Very not funny," Gabe said, fighting his irritation.

"How about *Harry Potter?*" She suggested.

"That sounds more like it."

Even though Annie remained withdrawn she still snuggled up to Gabe to watch the film, and as per usual he fell asleep half-way through it. She smiled at the familiarity and how much it meant to her. She watched him sleeping and felt tears stinging her eyes. He snorted and she smiled putting a hand protectively over her aching heart. She had never felt so exposed and vulnerable in her life. She was head over heels in love.

CHAPTER 34

The following morning Annie packed up a few essentials before heading in to work. Gabe was already hard at work, so she left a note for him to find on his noon break and headed out. She had a full day of clients ahead of her and wouldn't breath fresh air again until after seven this evening.

Someone had brought in donuts from the local bakery and there was a fresh pot of coffee waiting.

"You guys are the absolute best!" Annie exclaimed.

"Zoey is the one to thank," James said.

"Thank you, Zoey."

"Welcome," she said with her mouth full.

"How is the hunk?" Zoey asked.

"Don't want to talk about it," Annie said.

"Trouble in paradise?" J.J. asked.

"Just taking a little breather," Annie replied.

"Any more trouble from the asshole?" Zoey asked.

"Nope, I think I can close the book on that one."

"Just don't get too comfortable. I don't want you

living in fear the rest of your life but on the other hand, keep your eyes wide open," J.J. said.

"I will."

Annie's first customer arrived so she took a last gulp of coffee and went to greet them.

~

*G*abe sighed heavily, he wanted Annie back to stay for good. The house felt like a tomb without her. How had he ever managed to get out of bed before Annie came into his life? She was his muse, his breath, his light, he knew that he was ruined for any other woman, he had found his mate, his other half. There wasn't any question for him that he wanted to spend the rest of his life waking up with her beside him. He only hoped she'd come to the same conclusion. The sooner the better. He would try to talk her into a fancy date on Friday and tell her how he felt.

His offer for the farmhouse had been accepted, so now it was a matter of inspections and financing then he'd be moving. Without Annie none of it would matter. Her insecurity and jealousy were frustrating, but he supposed if it were reversed, he would want to smash the guy's face in. It wouldn't make him doubt her though.

Slapping a sandwich together, he sat at the kitchen table to eat and think about his busy day ahead and prioritize what needed to get done. Slim was back at work but on restrictions for another week. Cal was a real champ and had easily picked up the slack while Slim had been down. He wanted to squeeze in a longer session with Midnight today since the clock was ticking. Where had the time gone? He could hardly believe their time together was almost at an end.

Chugging his milk and then rinsing the glass, he rose to go face the rest of his day. Knowing that he wouldn't see Annie tonight was a bummer, but he had a lot to do to keep himself occupied. It was almost impossible to remember what his life had been like before Annie.

~

*A*nnie spent the next couple of nights ambling around her condo listlessly. *Damn him!* How the hell had she let this happen? She was miserable without him. She felt hollowed out. They were going on a date Friday night and Gabe had told her to dress up fancy. She had decided she would take the leap and tell him how she was feeling. The time apart, albeit painful, had given her a fresh perspective. This issue was clearly hers and not Gabe's. He had been honest and forthright about everything. She would have to get a grip on her insecurities and trust him if they were going to make it. There would always be beautiful women attracted to him. She turned out her bedside lamp and fell asleep thinking of Gabe's warm hands caressing her.

CHAPTER 35

*W*hat I wouldn't give fer a cigarette right about now. Jist can't get a good night of sleepin anymore. Ever since Slim had returned from the hospital he felt restless and tired at the same time. Glancing at the bedside clock he saw that it was only three a.m. He threw back the covers and got up; any hope of rest was a lost cause at this point. Gus, who had been curled up next to him sound asleep, looked at him and yawned.

"Ya got somin to say little fella?" The kitten stretched out and went back to snoozing.

Slim threw on his old jeans and stepped outside to get some fresh air. The stars were out in full tonight. Slim itched for a drag. He heard an owl off in the distance and then his ears perked up when he thought he heard a neigh coming from the barn. *That's strange, they should all be out in the pasture. I know I saw Gabe turnin em out.* He was going to ignore it then he heard a squeal and went to get his boots.

As he approached the barn, he caught a whiff of smoke and the hair stood up on the back of his old weathered neck. He walked straight through the barn toward the stalls where he had heard the squeals coming from. When he arrived, there was smoke and flames licking the back wall. He went into full alert.

He was startled to see the silhouette of a person through a haze of smoke. *Someone standing in the aisle at three a.m?*

"What the dang blame hell are you doing here? Why is that filly in her stall? She supossin to be out." Slim called out. "What ya doin here? Tresspassin? At least ya kin grab some buckets out of the stalls fill em up quick."

Slim saw the figure ahead of him lift an arm and shout, "No!" It was the last thing Slim heard before he was hit on the back of the head and fell to the ground unconscious.

⁓

Gabe woke up. Something wasn't right. He smelled smoke. With his windows open he could hear a horse squealing in the distance. He jumped out of bed and threw on some pants as he ran out the door. He almost collided with Sam who was heading in the same direction.

"What the fuck?" Gabe said.

In the distance Gabe could hear the sirens of an emergency vehicle approaching. "Did you call?" Gabe yelled as they ran into the barn.

"No," Sam replied.

The first thing Gabe saw through the smoke and

flames was a small crumpled figure lying in front of Midnight's stall.

"Slim!"

Gabe rushed over and grabbed Slim under his arms and hauled him out, which was easy as he weighed next to nothing. Sam rushed to Midnight's stall with flames darting all around, scorching them both and the smoke burning his lungs. He felt like it was a thousand degrees and he was breathing fire.

Midnight was rearing, her eyes rolling back in her terror. Sam managed to wrap a rope around her neck and pull as he talked soothingly, trying to get her out. She wouldn't budge. Fourteen hundred pounds of resistance. He didn't stand a chance. The fire was engulfing the barn now and he had seconds if that. He was praying for a miracle when Gabe ran back into the inferno.

"Give me the rope!" Gabe commanded. "Get outside and get some oxygen. *Now!*" he said as Sam protested. After pulling Slim to safety he had run back in for Sam and Midnight. It was the right call.

She was in full-on prey-animal panic, beyond communication. Gabe kept the alarm from his own voice as he spoke to her. When she realized it was Gabe, she immediately calmed, her ears moving back and forth, still terrified, but her trust in Gabe was absolute. Still prancing, she followed the man she had grown to trust and love out into the night and out of harm's way...she literally had walked through fire for Gabe.

Gabe could have cried with relief. The firefighters were now on-scene and battling the fire. The ambulance already had Slim on board and were leaving, sirens blaring. A second one had arrived, and they were currently forcing Sam to put on an oxygen mask for smoke inhalation. Sam was black with soot and his hair was singed pretty good. Overall, he didn't appear to have any severe burns.

Gabe was sure he looked similarly. Midnight's mane and tail were singed, and she had a pretty bad burn on her flank and rump areas. Gabe walked her over to the small paddock and would grab Whiskey for her company the first chance he got. The paramedics insisted that Gabe get some oxygen as a precaution, so he complied and wore the mask for a few minutes until he grew impatient with it.

Thank God Sam was a vet. Gabe knew how lucky he was that Midnight and Slim came out alive. He walked over to stand next to Sam, who was watching his barn burn to the ground. Once the fire took hold, it was amazing how quickly it went. At least the fire hadn't reached the houses or clinic, but the barn itself was destroyed. Swirling red lights lit the sky and bounced off the buildings, there was an eerie otherworldly feel and evil hung in the air.

Gabe put his arm around Sam's shoulder and said, "Barns can be rebuilt." Sam just nodded.

"I had so many memories made right there in that old barn. Dad and Mom before they were killed. Me and Casey, my first kiss…my first horse."

"The memories didn't burn down, you'll always have those," Gabe said.

The first police officer on the scene happened to be Ike, Bradley's partner. He briefly interviewed Sam and Gabe, and they made it clear that there was one suspect on their radar and that person was Bradley. He took their statements then went to his cruiser to put in a request to have an officer pick up his partner for questioning. Then he did one more thing, he called his friend to give him a heads up.

"Where are you right now?"

"At home in bed, where else would I be?"

"Are you sure?"

"What's this about Ike?"

"There has been a fire at the Parker Farm. Do you happen to know anything about that?"

"What the hell are you talking about?"

"Just what I said. You are sitting as their prime suspect right about now," Ike said.

"What the fuck!"

"Yeah, that's what I say. They are going to be knocking on your door any minute to bring you in for questioning." Ike said.

"I didn't do it! I swear! They will never believe me, and I have no alibi!"

Ike could hear the desperation in his friend's voice, "Don't do anything stupid. You'll get through this. I promise you. Come into the station, it's the only way to clear yourself. I'm calling you because we're friends and I believe in you," he said. He knew his friend hadn't been himself since Annie left, but a fire? Tack on murder or attempted murder at the very least. He sure as hell hoped his friend wasn't that far gone.

"I can't think…I have to go," he said and hung up the phone.

CHAPTER 36

"I want to check on Slim, but I'm worried about Midnight's burns," Gabe said to Sam.

"I'll tend to Midnight, you get cleaned up and go to Slim…and keep me posted."

"Sam will you be alright? I hate to leave you here alone."

"I'll call Darcy," he said.

"If you're sure…"

Gabe and Sam had calmed down the herd and as soon as it was possible had called the boarders to let them know what had happened. They'd build a shelter later that day. It would have to suffice until the new barn could be raised.

They hoped to not lose any boarders and since it was summer, the horses were out most of the time anyway. The loss was devastating. No indoor arena, no stalls, no hay, no tack or saddles, all destroyed. They were damn lucky that the houses weren't damaged and that no lives were lost.

Sam was heartbroken, and Gabe couldn't blame him, he felt it himself. He would make sure that they built a bigger and better barn for his friend. Sam had quite a few Amish clients in his veterinary practice and they were famous for throwing up quality barns in record time. It would get done as soon as possible. He would make sure of that.

~

*a*nnie woke up just as the sun rose. Something had disturbed her sleep. She opened her eyes and shrieked when she saw the outline of a man sitting in a club chair facing her. It took a moment for her eyes to adjust to the dawn light. *Bradley! Shit shit shit!*

"I'll bet you're surprised to see me here," he said, looking like someone who had escaped from a mental asylum. His hair was dirty and unkept, he was thin and gaunt, and his cheeks were hollowed out.

"I didn't do it. You have to tell them. It wasn't me!" he said in anguish.

"Didn't do what? I don't know what you're talking about."

"The barn, it burnt down. Your boyfriend told Ike it was me! They think I did it. Now there is an APB out for me."

"*No!*" Annie cried out. "I have to call Gabe," she said.

"Did you hear what I said? I didn't do it and they told the cops that it was me!"

"Please! I heard you, I'm listening but I have to know if everyone is alright."

"You can't change it anyway. What's done is done."

Annie suddenly noticed the gun sitting on his lap,

"Bradley if you didn't do anything wrong then why not turn yourself in? You're a cop for God's sake. You'll have every advantage."

"Annie, it's over. I've lost everything, the love of my life, my career, my reputation…there is no reason for me to be here anymore."

"Don't talk like that. You can get help!" Annie looked out of the corner of her eye at the phone sitting on her dresser charging. He noticed it at the same time.

"I don't have much time. This is one of the first places they'll look for me," Bradley said.

"I'll tell them that you didn't set the fire. Let me have my phone, I'll make the call now," Annie said.

He continued as if she hadn't spoken, "They won't even look for the person who did the crime. I'm the perfect scapegoat."

"That's not true. I'm certain that they want the person who is responsible. I know you must be completely out of your mind with fear, but if you can reason this out you'll see that your best bet is to call Ike and have him come get you and take you to the station for your statement."

"Oh Annie, all I ever wanted was for you to love me. I tried to give you everything you wanted. Now look at me, I'm ruined."

Annie's cell phone started ringing. *Gabe!* "Please, let me answer that. If I don't answer they will know something is wrong."

Bradley rose from the chair and sat next to Annie on the edge of the bed. Taking her hand, his eyes blazing with intensity, he insisted, "Annie, I need you to listen. I'm here to say goodbye. I've fucked everything up. I wanted you to know that I'm sorry for everything and I will always love you."

"Bradley, please turn yourself in, clear your name."

"I don't want to be a cop anymore. I'm done, finished."

"Where are you going? What will you do?"

"I don't know yet, but don't let them pin this on me. Push them to find the real arsonist. Promise me?"

"I'll do what I can."

Bradley stood up, "I guess this is goodbye. I'm sorry Annie, I love you. Please forgive me."

Then he was gone.

CHAPTER 37

Gabe had called Annie, but she didn't pick up. He didn't want to leave a message of this import, so he hung up. Entering Slim's hospital room, he eyed all of the monitors warily. He had talked to Pepper, whose shift was ending soon; she had been here when he was admitted. She said Slim hadn't regained consciousness yet, but his vitals were stable. Probably a concussion and hopefully the swelling would be minimal.

He looked impossibly frail to Gabe. When had Slim become so important to him? Why was he suddenly terrified of losing this crotchety old man? Somewhere along the line, Slim had become more than an employee, he had become a friend, maybe even family.

Pepper came in, still in her nurse's uniform. She put her arm around Gabe and said, "He'll pull through this. He's a tough old bird."

"Even with what he just went through with his heart and all?"

"Even with all that," Pepper said encouragingly.

"I hope you're right."

"Hey, have a little faith, I am a nurse you know," she said teasing him. "The police were here trying to get his statement. They obviously left empty-handed."

"That can wait. They are looking for Bradley as we speak. I know it was him. Who else could it be?"

"He is the most obvious, but you never know. How is Sam taking all of this?"

"He looked completely beaten down. All he has worked for…"

"It sucks but at least no lives were lost He'll be okay. He'll rebuild."

"That's what I told him, too. I'm sure he's in shock."

"Who wouldn't be. How are you holding up?"

"Honestly I don't have a clue. Right now, I'm going through the motions."

"One foot in front of the other," Pepper agreed.

"I'm going to sit here with Slim for a while," Gabe said.

"I'll check in later after I get some sleep. It was a long shift."

"Bye Pepper."

"See ya Gabe."

Gabe sat down and leaned back in the uncomfortable hospital chair and promptly fell asleep to the steady beeping of the cardiac monitor. He awoke to a gentle kiss on his forehead. "Annie!"

"I heard. The fire! Thank God you're okay." She glanced over at Slim, "Any changes with Slim's condition?"

"No. Annie." '

"Gabe," they both started talking at the same time.

"Me first," Annie said. "I owe you an apology. What happened the other day is totally on me. I can't put you in a cage away from the rest of the world. My insecurities are my responsibility, not yours. I'm so sorry. You didn't deserve to be treated that way."

"Thank you for that." The magnitude of what happened began to sink in. "The barn is gone," he said, voice breaking.

Annie held Gabe's head against her belly, stroking his hair, "When I think of what could have happened to you, with the fire, it makes me feel like throwing up. I'm sick."

"Midnight, the rest of the herd, are all okay. Hopefully Slim will pull through."

"God, I hope so. It must have been terrifying." She glanced over at Slim and felt her eyes misting up. "He looks so fragile."

"We're all fragile when it comes right down to it," Gabe said solemnly.

"There's another thing, I hate to bring up right now but I feel you should know," Annie said.

"Okay."

"*U*m, I don't know how to say this without freaking you out, but Bradley showed up at my house before dawn. I was startled awake and there he was," she said.

"That son of…"

"No wait—" she held up a hand, "—hear me out. He swears he didn't set the fire, and he knows that he is the prime suspect. I believe him. He apologized for everything he wants us to find the person who set the fire."

"How can you believe a word he says? I don't get it."

"I just know. I could tell. He didn't smell like smoke, he wasn't covered in soot, he looked like he hadn't bathed for days, he was unkempt and haggard but not from just coming from burning down a barn. It came from being eaten up from the inside."

"You'll have to let the police know about his visit. It's not up to us to clear him."

"I know but hopefully when I tell them everything I know, they'll look into it deeper and not make assumptions that it was Bradley," she said.

"If it wasn't him then who? I just hope they find the bastard that did this," he rubbed the back of his neck the fatigue setting in. "I need to get back to the farm," Gabe said, reluctant to leave Slim and even more so Annie.

Annie kissed Gabe then got up from his lap. "I canceled all of my appointments for the rest of the day. I'd like to sit here with Slim for a while. I'll stop by the farm later."

"Yes. By the way, some good news, my offer on the house was accepted. It should be mine in month or so," Gabe said.

"Congratulations."

"Annie?"

"Yes."

"You'll stay with me tonight?"

"Yes."

"See you later then," Gabe said, then paused as if he wanted to say more then changed his mind. He kissed her again then left.

Annie settled down to wait for Slim to wake up.

~

*G*abe returned to the farm and found Sam and Cal already in full swing, building the shelter overhang area for the horses to stand under. He immediately picked up some tools and joined in.

"What's the word on Slim?" Cal asked.

"No change, still in a coma," Gabe said.

Cal shook his head sadly and said, "Any idea of the prognosis?"

"Not really. Pepper thinks he'll pull through, but just coming off that heart procedure and being so frail, I'm not convinced."

"Annie said Bradley paid her a visit in the early hours and claims he didn't set the fire. She believes him. I trust her judgement...so, if not him then who?"

"The million-dollar question," Sam said.

They worked silently for quite some time, each deep into their own thoughts until Cal said, "I hate to leave you guys to all of this work alone, but I have to be somewhere in about an hour. I'm going to have to take off now, so I have time to go home and clean up."

"Will you be back later today? It's kind of bad timing," Gabe said. "We really need the extra hand."

"I'll try my best. I have a doctor's appointment. I've been having some stomach issues," he explained.

"Can't stop ya, hopefully it's nothing serious."

"I've had this appointment for a while, it took forever to get in, sorry about the timing."

"Hopefully we'll see ya back here after," Gabe said.

"I'll do my best."

After Cal took off Sam and Gabe continued with their project. All Gabe could see was Slim laying in that hospital bed and it made him feel powerless. *Please let him pull through this.*

~

*D*arcy showed up with lunch, so they took a break. Concern for Sam was etched onto her face as she watched him wearily go through the motions of eating his sandwich. He looked bone tired and it broke her heart. Sam was always the upbeat one. He was always so cheerful and full of life that it made his grief that much more obvious.

When they were done eating, Darcy picked up a hammer and pitched in to help. It felt good to be performing a task, pounding nails helped to vent some of her anger. They hadn't been at it too long when Annie joined them.

Gabe put down his drill and grabbed Annie's arm, pulling her roughly against his chest. "Don't ever leave me again," he growled against her lips.

He devoured her mouth as she clung to him, both needing the comfort of touch. Coming up for air, he studied her before planting kisses all over her face— creamy skin, plump lips, half-closed eyes...he returned to her mouth and covered it with his own.

Annie put her hands on either side of his face, her fingertips touching his hair, she looked deep into his passionate eyes, "I won't, I promise."

"I'll keep you to that."

Clearing his throat, Sam politely reminded them they weren't the only ones there. Darcy laughed and said, "So glad you could join us Annie."

Annie looked around at the devastation shaking her head sadly, "Who could do such a thing?"

"We're all asking the same thing," Darcy said. "How's Slim? Any changes?"

"No, Pepper showed up, so I left. What can I do to help?"

Nodding toward the red toolbox, Sam said, "Grab a hammer."

Annie did and soon they were all busy pounding, drilling, measuring, sawing, relieved to have the distraction and a purpose. Her arms ached from wielding the hammer, but it somehow felt good.

They all worked with intensity, pouring all of their pent-up emotions into this project. Rebuilding somehow empowered each one of them. They were looking to the future and moving forward from this destruction. Rising from the ashes they would heal and persevere.

CHAPTER 38

*P*epper glanced up when Cal entered the hospital room. "How is he?" Cal asked.

"Unfortunately, about the same. Sometimes these brain injuries take time. Don't give up on him just yet."

"Wouldn't dream of it," he said, smiling sadly.

"Since you're here to take a shift I think I'll take a break and go home for a few hours."

"No problem. I'll stay a while."

Pepper stretched her arms over head as she stood to leave. "I'll never understand why they can't have comfortable chairs in hospital rooms. It's a pet peeve of mine."

"Be the change," he said.

"Very funny. Don't think I haven't tried."

"Knowing you, I'm sure of it."

"I'll catch you later then. If there is any change give me a ring," Pepper said scribbling down her number.

"Sure, see ya."

"Later."

Cal settled in and sat staring at Slim, watching the monitors keep track of his vitals like statisticians. He wasn't aware of time passing as he waited. His cell phone pinged, and he read the text. He took one last look at Slim then headed down to the foyer.

"Follow me," Cal said.

Cal and Kip entered the room quietly.

"Stand outside the room, this won't take long, alert me if anyone comes close," Kip said.

"I still think you should wait and see how this turns out on its own. He probably won't pull through anyway. I like the old coot. I didn't sign up for this," Cal said.

"I don't pay you to think. Just do as you're told."

"You," said Slim in a small weak voice. "Yer nothing but scum, I saw yer at the barn, it was you," he said faintly, looking right at Cal.

"You were at the wrong place at the wrong time. Too bad you couldn't mind your own business." Kip said coldly. "Unfortunately, you have become a loose end that needs to be tied up."

Slim tried to yell, but his voice was too weak, and it came out little more than a whispered, "Help."

"You call that a scream? Nobody likely to hear that and come running," Kip said. "What are you waiting for?" he snarled at Cal.

"I'm having second thoughts Kip; a fire was one thing but murder?"

"Get your fucking ass out in the hall *now*!"

Cal reluctantly left the room and Kip approached Slim with a syringe in his hand. "You won't feel a thing. You'll just go to sleep and die knowing you had a good long life. Nobody will be the wiser. It's just too bad you had to go and wake up."

Slim pressed the nurse's button and ripped the IV out of his arm, causing the alarm to go off. "You're an old fool, don't fight it," Kip snarled. A struggle ensued but Slim had no strength and knew this was the end of the road for him.

Suddenly the door burst open and a security guard ran in with two nurses right behind him. "Put the syringe down and your hands up!"

Kip charged the guard, knocking him into the two nurses, who all lost their balance and went crashing onto the floor. The guard quickly scrambled to his feet and set chase. The nurses recovered and went to Slim's side.

Kip had almost reached the stairwell when Cal stepped in front of him and blocked his exit. It was just enough time for the guard to catch up and with Cal's help they managed to restrain him.

"You're going to pay," Kip said ominously.

"There's no doubt about that, but one day when I die, I won't have to meet my maker as a murderer. I'll take my chances with your wrath," Cal said.

Backup was already on its way thanks to Cal's last-minute attack of conscience. In the end he had grown attached to Slim, really everyone at the farm, and he hadn't been able to go through with it. He knew he would have to pay for his sins, but fortunately no lives had been lost and he was grateful for that.

⁓

Since Slim had no next of kin, Pepper and Gabe's phone numbers had been given to be notified of any changes in Slims condition. Pepper got the first call and immediately headed back to the hospital. Annie and Gabe arrived right behind her. They all rushed to Slim's room where they were stopped just outside his door.

A police officer stood guard, causing the three to look at each other with concern. "What's going on? I'm a nurse here and a good friend of the patient. Can I get in to see him?"

"The police are in questioning him right now. If you show me your hospital ID I can let you in. Just you though."

She pulled the cord out from under her shirt and showed him her credentials.

"Go on in then."

Pepper looked back at Gabe and Annie and said, "I'll keep you posted."

"We'll be in the waiting room down the hall. Come get us the minute we can see Slim," Gabe said.

"Of course."

Pepper entered the room and felt like crying when she saw Slim awake and talking to the investigators. He looked like he weighed about one hundred pounds soaking wet and he was as pale as a ghost, but he was alive, and awake, and talking.

"Slim, thank God!" she said interrupting the officer to rush to Slims side and gently hug him. "We've been so worried."

"Ya hain't getting rid of me that easy," he said, his voice a smidgeon above a whisper.

Pepper wiped her eyes, smiling through her tears. "You have no idea how happy I am to hear that."

The officers had politely stepped back for the reunion but were now ready to wrap up their interrogation. "Virgil, we have your statement, if we have any more questions, we'll get back with you. You've been most helpful. Concentrate on getting stronger, ya hear?" Officer Connie Gibbons said.

"Thank ya," he said weakly.

They both nodded to Pepper and left the room.

"Virgil?" Pepper said.

"Ferget you ever heard that," he grinned, weakly as if even that took too much strength.

"I don't think I can," she smiled at her friend. "But I can keep it between you and me." She winked.

"I promised to go and get Gabe and Annie after the police left. I'll be right back."

"I hain't goin nowhere I reckin."

When Pepper went to find Gabe and Annie, they were right outside of the waiting room, talking with Officer Gibbons.

"Fill me in," Pepper said.

"It was Cal, all along." Gabe said unable to disguise the shock and hurt from his voice.

"Cal? No way!"

"Yes way," Annie said.

"What, why, how?" Pepper sputtered.

"They don't have all of the facts nailed down, but apparently it was a scam to collect on insurance money. Midnight was supposed to perish in the fire and Cal's boss was going to cash in. We'll know more later. Seems as if Slim was a witness and had to be silenced. Cal had a last-minute change of heart and couldn't go through with it."

"Through with what?"

"They came here to the hospital to finish him off." Gabe said.

"What? Oh my God! Thank you, baby Jesus, that they failed!" Pepper exclaimed. "I'm in shock. Cal was beginning to feel like family."

"Tell me about it," Annie said. "I went out one night, and I met a couple of guys from Kentucky at a bar, said they were here on business. Later that week I ran into Cal sitting at the diner talking with them. He claimed he didn't know them, random run in with fellow Kentuckians. I'm certain it was connected to this. At the time I didn't give it much thought."

"Wow, arson, attempted murder, insurance fraud… my head is going to explode," Pepper said.

"I must be nine kinds of a fool," Gabe said.

"Don't even go there! We were all fooled. Quintessential all-American guy: warm, charismatic boy next door. He had his act down," Pepper said.

"I'm still in shock," Annie said. "To think I danced and partied with him while all the time he was up to no good. It does kind of make you doubt your ability to discern truth from lies. I thought he really cared about us."

"Yeah me too," Gabe said glumly.

"Let's go back and visit with Slim for a little while," Annie suggested.

Slim had his eyes closed when they entered the room but when Gabe touched his arm, they flew open. They shared a moment of connection as Gabe squeezed his bony arm and said, "Slim I gotta tell ya, you had me pretty scared there. I'm glad you're back to the land of the living."

"When that feller was comin at me with that there syringe, I knew I was goin be meetin my maker. Gots to admit, I weren't ready jist yet. I tried tellin ya, I jist didn't like im. Somin weren't right about im." Slim closed his eyes, his face still deathly pale.

"I should have listened," Gabe said quietly.

"I was lookin' at his file whenever you came in yer office and caught me red-handed."

"Ah, I had forgotten about that."

"It jist didn't add up fer me. Too much of a fluke, him showin up at the perfect time and all, with all yer boxes checked, and he was too slick."

"Slim, from now on you're doing all of the interviews and hiring," Gabe said.

"I reckin."

The nurse popped her head in and said she had to chart him and check his vitals then they were taking him down for another scan.

"We'll be here when you get back Slim," Gabe said.

Annie reached into her pocket and pulled out the four-leaf clover he had given her and handed it to Slim. "Here why don't you hold onto this for a bit. It sure has worked for me."

He grinned and took it from her. "It kint hurt me none."

Pepper leaned down and whispered in Slims ear, "See ya Virgil," and kissed his cheek which, much to everyone's surprise, brought a rosy blush to Slim's cheeks.

CHAPTER 39

With Kip and Cal in custody they were booked for insurance fraud, arson, and attempted murder. The captain hoped to reach Bradley to share the news so that he would know he was off the hook. His call went straight to voicemail, so he enlisted Ike to keep trying to reach his partner.

Cal cooperated fully and had confessed to his part in everything. He had fingered Kip and Roy who were the masterminds of the insurance fraud scheme to cash in on Midnight's misfortune in order to pay off Kip's massive gambling debts. Since Kip had only forty-nine percent interest in Imperial Farms, his partner would have to be investigated as well. But Cal assured the authorities that the Bartell family, Kips partners, were completely in the dark about the scheme. The whole point had been to replace the embezzled funds before they had discovered them missing.

By Cal's account, Kip had acted on his own and devised a plan after running into deep gambling debt.

Since he felt Midnight was a long shot for rehabilitation, he had decided to sacrifice her life for the million-dollar insurance payoff. They found a relative unknown newcomer to the training world, Gabe, that wouldn't have the experience to question or the security set-up to interfere with their plan. The fire had been a last resort after multiple attempts, by Cal, to sabotage Midnights health.

It was dumb luck that Gabe had to hire another hand. In stepped Cal. Cal had the decency to look ashamed as he admitted that he agreed to participate for the hundred thousand-dollar payoff that Kip had promised him. It was likely that Cal would be released on bond since he was cooperating, but Kip and Roy would likely stay behind bars for a long time to come.

$\sim$

The next day a guard came to Cal's cell and said, "You've got a visitor."

"Gabe Hunter?"

"Yep, only one on your visitor's list."

Cal had requested the visit but was dreading it. He reluctantly followed the guard to the secure meeting room. There was Gabe, sitting at a table. Cal sat down across from him.

"You wanted to see me?" Gabe asked.

"Yeah, Gabe, I don't expect you to understand or forgive me, but I needed to tell you my side."

"You're right, I'll never understand. For starters, how could anyone try to harm an innocent animal? Midnight had already been through so much and was completely dependent on us. How?" Gabe said.

"I know…"

"Then to worm your way into our lives, we treated you like family, man how sick does someone have to be to fake it so damn good?"

"I know, I deserve everything you can dish out, but when I was offered a hundred thousand from my Uncle Kip to do the job, I didn't know any of ya. I didn't even know the horse for that matter. It just seemed like an easy way to make a hundred grand."

"You're a piece of shit. Slim had your number from day one and I didn't listen, for that I can't forgive myself."

Cal said quietly, "I just wanted you to know that in the end I couldn't go through with it. I grew to care about all of you. Especially you Gabe. You're the first man I've ever looked up to. You're strong and honest and fair, you have integrity and honor. I wished I could be like you. I'm sorry that I realized all this too late."

Gabe shook his head sadly. "I'm sorry too. I really liked you, I trusted you. I guess I've never been motivated by money so it's impossible for me to fathom how that could seduce a person to commit such acts."

"I want you to know that I'm cooperating fully with the investigation. My uncle will be going away for a long time and I'll probably have some years behind bars to think about things."

"Why did you wait so long to do the right thing?"

"What started out as a fantasy in my mind, a money grab, became something else entirely in real life. By the time I realized the true consequences I was in too deep. I found a family and people I cared about. I know it's lame and will never be enough, but I'm most sorry that I betrayed a man I grew to respect."

"Respected me so much you tried to destroy everything that mattered to me."

"When it all went down in the barn that night, Slim surprised us, I yelled for Kip to stop but he knocked Slim out and left him to die. I tried to pull him out, but Kip stopped me. He had a gun, I had no choice but to go along."

"And to lock Midnight in a stall to burn to death? What kind of person could do that?"

Cal had no answer, he just hung his head.

"You didn't have to come here today, I thank ya for that," Cal said.

Gabe stood up and walked out of the meeting without saying another word.

CHAPTER 40

*A*nnie found Gabe out in the paddock with Midnight. He looked so forlorn that her heart hurt. She quietly walked up to them and put her arm around Gabe's waist. "Babe I came to pull you away for dinner. Hi Midnight," she said.

Midnight sniffed her outreached hand looking for treats. "I just happen to have what you're looking for," she said pulling out an oat cookie.

"They're coming to get her this Friday," Gabe said.

"I know that's going to hurt like hell."

"I knew it had to happen eventually, but I didn't expect it to be so damn hard."

"Your bond is special. You saved her Gabe. She knows that. For that you have to feel good. If it weren't for you, she might have been put down. You gave her life back to her."

"She gave me so much more than I ever did for her."

"I'm sure they would let you visit her," Annie said.

"Now that's a thought," he said, smiling for the first time in a while.

"She will always be in your heart. That won't leave with her." She grabbed Gabe's hand and said, "Let's go eat."

"I have to let Whiskey in the paddock with Midnight and throw them each a flake of hay. I'll be right along."

"Don't take too long or things will be cold," Annie said. "Bye Midnight."

~

*A*nnie watched Gabe pick at his meal. She tried to make conversation, "I heard that they were finally able to reach Bradley."

"Oh yeah? How did that go?"

"Apparently he's in Florida and has no intention of returning to Michigan. He is bartending, of all things. Says he feels free for the first time in years and he wants to keep it that way," Annie smiled.

"At least he is out of your hair and stripped of his power."

"He really wasn't cop material," she said in agreement. "Since no charges were filed against him by Sam, and he quit the force, he really is free."

Annie got up and cleared the table. She had started a fire in the fireplace and said, "Let's go snuggle by the fire and watch a light movie, what do you think?"

"Sure."

"Let Annie make it all better," she teased.

They sprawled out on the couch together, her back to his chest, Gabe hugging her tightly against him. He kissed her neck then began to nibble.

"That tickles," she said giggling.

In response he moved to her ear and whispered, "I love you Annie Morgan."

Annie's eyes widened and she became completely still, hardly daring to breath. "Ah could you repeat that please?"

"Only if you turn to face me."

She turned over only to lose herself in the warmth of his gaze. Breathlessly she said, "Now, you were saying?"

"They are predicting highs in the eighties tomorrow, with sunny skies..." he couldn't contain his laughter as her eyes narrowed and looked like twin flames about to sear him. She began to tickle him knowing just where his most vulnerable spot was.

"Okay, okay, I love you alright?"

"That's what I thought you said." And she rolled back over.

"What? That's it?"

Now the table were turned, and he squeezed her against him, "Why you little..."

She quickly turned in his arms and planted a kiss on his open mouth. "For the record, I love you too."

"Now that's more like it. Babe, I don't know what I did to deserve you but whatever it was I'm glad for it," Gabe said.

"You deserve everything good."

He reached under her shirt to massage her breast and she groaned. Tugging her tee shirt over her head he tossed it aside and pulled her bra strap down, kissing her bare shoulder. Gabe hooked his index finger inside the lacy bra, he drew it down over her breast, and lowered his mouth to take her nipple. "You have the most beautiful body I've ever seen. Your breasts are every man's fantasy," he said, fully aroused.

Suckling gently at first, at her urging he tugged harder with his lips and tongue, sucking, drawing her engorged nipple further into his mouth, while kneading her other breast.

Wild with longing, she cried out, "Gabe, please!"

He moved to her mouth and kissed her deeply then, keeping his eyes locked with hers, he pulled her tights down over her long thighs. Kissing his way up her inner thighs, he lingered over the soft skin near her apex, his tongue trailing fire wherever it touched. Her delicious scent made him want to take her like a wild animal. She bucked under his skilled love making.

He stood and removed his jeans and underwear, his body perfectly sculpted. Annie was transfixed by his throbbing penis. His thighs were muscular and strong. His belly flat. The thin line of hair running from his navel to his phallus made her crazy with desire. She watched as he reached for the end table drawer and pulled out a condom. She pulled her panties off and released her bra.

"Let me just look at you," he said. Gazing at this exquisite creature, now naked and fully aroused, did something to him. She was wild in her abandon. Completely comfortable with her body and her sexuality she stretched sensually almost like a cat. Then she lifted her pelvis thrusting it toward him in a seductive motion, opening her thighs wide. Her womanhood was on full display for him, her pink, swollen labia, her creamy thighs, her mound of hair, he was lost. He had to have her. Mounting he thrust deeply inside as her legs wrapped around him. He pumped hard and fast. Both climaxing within seconds.

CHAPTER 41

$\mathcal{T}$he barn-building jam was in full swing. There were over a dozen men working on it not including Sam and Gabe, who pitched in when they could. The indoor arena and stall were now under roof. It was only a matter of a week or two before it was completed.

Gabe was riding Midnight in the outdoor arena when the large horse trailer drove up the lane. They were early. He had a lump the size of an apple in his throat as he dismounted. "Come on girl, your chariot awaits." Her ears twitched in response.

He removed her saddle and bridal and secured her lead rope to the hitching post the went to greet the Bartells.

"I'm Gabe, welcome to Parker Farms."

"Hi. I'm Doug and this is my wife Sue," he said offering his hand.

Sue said, "We had to come ourselves to offer our

sincerest apologies. We still feel in shock about what happened. We know you have been informed that we were cleared of any wrong-doing, but we still feel responsible somehow."

"I'm sure, but we don't hold you responsible. The person who did it is going away for a long time. That's what matters."

"We saw you riding Midnight. She hardly looks like the same filly that left Imperial Farms," Doug said. "I'm very impressed. Looks like her burns are healing nicely."

"Thanks to Sam," Gabe said.

"We'd like it if you would consider training more of our horses in the future. I would certainly understand if you decided to cut your ties with us but…"

"I'd be honored, sir," Gabe said.

"Call me Doug, please," he said.

"And I'm Sue."

"Come take a look at the new barn, it's coming right along. I'll introduce you to Sam Parker."

Sam was hanging from a rafter when they entered under the cavernous roof.

"Hey, come on down and meet the Bartells."

Sam quickly climbed down and joined them. "Sam Parker, welcome."

"We're not just here to take Midnight back, but also to offer our apologies and to present you with a check, to cover anything extra the insurance might not pick up."

"You don't need to do that," Sam argued. "Our community has come together in a big way. The local Amish order know how to build a barn and that's what they've done. Look at it!"

"Pretty amazing, but we insist. Consider it a

donation toward the animals' wellbeing...any future rescues, or horse retirees, or bonuses for your hired hands." He thrust the check at Sam. When Sam looked down at the amount he whistled.

"That's mighty generous of ya," Sam said. "There's someone I'd like ya to meet. He got knocked out and left in the burning barn for dead. You just gave me an idea that has convinced me to reconsider your offer. Maybe I was a little too hasty saying no. I've never had fulltime employees until the last couple of years, but as my responsibilities grew, I've added a manager and an invaluable ranch hand."

Slim was sitting on a lawn chair supervising the barn construction when they approached. "Slim, meet the owners of Imperial Farms," Sam said.

Slim tipped his cowboy hat but remained silent.

"They have generously offered to start up a retirement account in your name for what you went through."

Slim's eyes widened then he said to Sam, "You sure you hain't tryin to tell me sumthin?' I still have a few good years left in me I reckin."

"I sure hope so," Gabe said.

"Well that's mighty generous of youin's but I can't accept it."

"Slim you don't have much choice in the matter. I'll be opening an account in your name, case closed."

"Please Slim, it would ease our burden tremendously if you'd accept it. We feel so horrible about what our partner did. It's a small way for us to make up for his despicable behavior," Sue said. "You would be doing us the favor."

Slim stayed silent, his wheels turning. "I reckin the

one hurtin the most would be our Gabe here. He fell head over heels fer that there filly of yours. She fer him too."

"They looked pretty solid when we drove up," Doug said.

"Its prit near magic," Slim said.

"Speaking of Midnight, I'd better go prepare her," Gabe said, feeling like he'd been punched in the gut at the reminder of why they were here.

He left the Bartells and went to say his final goodbye to Midnight. Choking up he said, "Listen to me girl and listen good, you're going to be fine, ya hear me? It will take a little time to adjust but before you know it, you'll be finding your way. On to the next adventure," he put his arms around her neck and breathed in her scent. Annie came up behind Gabe and wrapped her arms around him. He swiped at his eyes.

"I love you Gabe Hunter. You are a good man."

"I love you too Annie."

The Bartells, witnessing all this, exchanged a look, and Doug nodded at his wife in agreement. "Gabe, seeing all that Midnight has been through in her young life and how well she's thriving here, would you consider keeping her? We kind of think another transition would be too much for her. We just don't have the heart to do that to her again."

"Are you kidding me?"

"No. We're dead serious," Doug said.

"Yes! I'll train your next dozen horses free of charge!"

"That won't be necessary," Sue said. "We want you to have her. You've all been through so much because of us it's the least we can do. With her burns she wouldn't be able to show anymore anyway. With the trauma she has been through…well we just think its best."

"I don't know what to say or how to thank you, but you have made me the happiest man on the planet right about now!"

"That's wonderful!" Annie said, clapping her hands and practically squealing with delight. "You have no idea what you have just done! Thank you." Without thinking she threw her arms around Sue for a big hug.

"That's settled then. We'll take our leave, and you'll be hearing from us soon." They took off hauling their empty trailer, with Gabe practically in shock.

"Hear that Midnight? You get to stay!"

"Oh my God! Did that really just happen?" Annie said.

Slim walked up and said, "I see they left somethin' behind."

"Did you intentionally plant that seed?"

"I hain't that powerful, but fer sure it was the right thing fer them to do."

"I agree one hundred percent Slim! With my Irish blood I might be a wee bit superstitious, but I believe that shamrock you whittled for me has some hidden powers."

Slim grinned, tipped his hat and left.

"He's a mystery that one," Annie said.

"I love that old timer."

"He has certainly grown on me as well," Annie said. "I have to get back to work, I just stopped by to check on you."

"Thanks for that."

"Call me later?" she asked.

"Yep." Gabe leaned down for a quick kiss then she was gone.

CHAPTER 42

"*I*'ll wash, you dry," Annie said.

"You always get to wash," Gabe said.

"You big baby, I do not."

"Since you cooked, I guess it's your call. Just remember, drying counts as two chores since the one wielding the dish towel has to put them away."

"Noted," Annie said dryly.

"I've got a surprise for you after we're done here," Gabe said.

"I hate surprises, what is it?"

"Not telling."

"You're just trying to get back at me."

"Hurry up and wash, time's a-wasting."

Gabe put the final dish away and grabbed the keys to his truck, "Hurry up, let's go."

"I'm ready, I just have to find my flip flops." Slipping on the bright pink sandals, she followed Gabe to the truck.

"Close your eyes," he instructed. "No peeking, I mean it."

"I promise."

They drove for several minutes and then came to stop.

"Open your eyes."

Annie did and she shrieked, "It's yours!"

"Yep. As of yesterday, I am now the proud owner of my first home. Let's go," he said, dangling the house keys in front of her.

They walked up the stairs to the large wraparound porch leading to the front door. "Wait, come over here," Gabe said, pulling Annie away from peering in the front window.

"Gabe! I'm too heavy," she said, laughing as he picked her up into his arms.

"Yeah right." He easily cradled her to him, while unlocking the front door. "It's only right that I carry you over the threshold."

"You are so romantic, that's one of my favorite things about you," Annie said, dimpling.

He pushed the door open and they entered. "It's even grander than I remember," Annie said. "Those old beams, the floors, its fabulous."

"I bought a bottle of wine, it's in the fridge, why don't you go pour us a glass and we'll have a toast."

Annie practically skipped to the kitchen, opening the fridge she spied the bottle of wine, then she saw a brown paper bag with her name on it. Curious she peered inside and saw a small black velvet box. Her heart began to race. Gabe entered the room and said, "Whatcha' got there?" He reached for the bag.

Annie's eyes were shimmering with unshed tears

and as she looked at Gabe he got down on one knee. Pulling out the jeweler's box, he opened it and held it toward her, "Annie Morgan, I knew you were the girl for me on that first trail ride we took, will you put me out of my misery and say that you'll marry me?"

"*Yes!*"

He took the sparkling diamond out of the box as she held out her hand. He slipped the ring on her finger and kissed it. Standing, he picked her up and swung her around as she laughed and cried at the same time.

"We are going to have such a grand adventure together Annie. Can't you just see us ten years from now, twenty, thirty, first little rug rats of our own, then seeing them off to college, then us with gray hair and grandchildren!"

"Whoa, stop, I don't want to miss today," she said, laughing at his joy.

"I love you so much Annie girl."

"I love you too Gabe, with all of my heart."

"I think we should initiate the farmhouse and begin working on that family we were just talking about."

"I think that sounds like an excellent idea." Annie looked down at the diamond ring surrounded with glittering green emeralds. "It's beautiful!"

"I'm looking at beautiful, and I'll never grow tired of it." He nuzzled into her neck and nipped playfully.

Annie warmed with desire and anticipation. "Now about that family plan…"

The End for Now…

ACKNOWLEDGMENTS

I'd like to thank April Wilson for sharing her wisdom, her encouragement and her continued support. Her generosity of spirit is inspiring!

Thanks to the other April in my literary world, April Bennet, my editor and guide for *More Than a Fling*. Her empathy, humor and smarts are everything I could ever have asked for.

BOOKS BY JILL DOWNEY

THE HEARTLAND SERIES:

More Than A Boss

More Than A Memory

More Than A Fling

Can't not
How can I not love you:
Soundtrack
Jay Enrequis

Printed in Great Britain
by Amazon